THE CONSUMERS

DOMINIC R. DANIELS & DOUG K. OWEN

Dedicated to
Phil & Mary Daniels

INT. SECRET LAB - NIGHT

The lab is full of various science equipment: microscopes, chemical racks, 90's computers, and a gurney.

Several people in lab coats are at their stations, looking at the gurney. From a nearby door, in walk H.G. GOLDEN and TED STEINBERG. Several other scientists are with them, as well as an old man, RODNEY MONGAN.

Ted assists Rodney onto the gurney and straps him down, as H.G. preps a syringe with a viscous fluid.

RODNEY

What are these straps for?

TED STEINBERG

Sorry Rodney, just in case.

H.G. turns on a handheld tape recorder. The room goes silent.

> H.G. GOLDEN
>
> Date is October 4, 1990. Approximately eleven PM. Subject is age seventy-five, male, Caucasian, health deteriorating. Subject shows advanced signs of aging, wrinkles, some mental deterioration.

> RODNEY
>
> I'm in the room, ya know.

H.G. turns to him.

> H.G. GOLDEN
>
> Relax. You're about to make history. Enjoy the moment.

> RODNEY
>
> Can you dope me up already? I'm not getting any younger. Yet.

> H.G. GOLDEN
> (into the recorder)
>
> Now administering twenty ccs of the first batch of Eden, Mark One.

H.G. injects the subject with the formula. A baited breath as all in the room wait to see what happens.

CLOSE ON RODNEY - Wrinkles and lines begin to disappear.

INSERT –

INT. RODNEY'S BODY
Among floating white and red blood cells, new proteins are being generated in his body.

BACK TO SCENE -
Rodney sighs with some relief. Some of the scientists applaud. Ted and H.G. smile.

H.G. GOLDEN (CONT'D)
The serum is working.

But the celebration is short-lived as moments later -
Rodney emits a blood-curdling SCREAM!
He begins to spasm, his veins begin to bulge, and he coughs up blood everywhere. His skin begins to melt into a red, pulpy mass as he becomes increasingly delirious with pain.
He shrieks and convulses violently, breaking out of the gurney straps and stumbling off the table. Several SCIENTISTS head for the door in a panic. One of them trips on the ground and is grabbed by the monster that was Rodney. The Scientist screams in disgust and fear.

SCIENTIST #2
Hold him down! Get the Thorazine!

Monster Rodney claws at First Scientist's throat, ripping his neck wide open. Blood splatters like a volcano. Panic ensues as some scientists try to subdue the creature.
Rodney fights back, wildly swinging his deformed limbs. H.G. approaches the creature with a syringe of sedatives.

H.G. GOLDEN
Hold him! Hold him!

The creature bites into H.G.'s shoulder, through his lab coat. Blood gushes from the wound. He SCREAMS in pain.
Ted tries to pull the creature off and it knocks Ted back into a table. The creature then turns to Ted and moves in for the kill. Ted fumbles, throwing chemicals and other apparatuses around, reaching for a bottle of sulfuric acid.

He throws it in Rodney's face and the creature writhes in agony as the front of its skull melts away. Its brains SLAP onto the floor. Ted gets up, frozen in disbelief.

                    TED STEINBERG
          Jesus Christ!

Several others look on at what just happened. H.G. gets to his feet, holding his bleeding shoulder.

                    H.G. GOLDEN
          Ted, are you alright?

                    TED STEINBERG
          Henry, he's dead.

                    H.G. GOLDEN
          Listen to me! It's gonna be alright!

                    TED STEINBERG
          What are we gonna do? We have to call the police!

                    H.G. GOLDEN
          No way! We're not going to jail over this. It was an
          accident!

The other scientists tend to their wounds. H.G. looks around at them, then back to Ted.

                    H.G. GOLDEN (CONT'D)
          An accident! These things happen. We will forfeit our
          grant, clean this up, and we will all keep our mouths
          shut, got it?

The other scientists in the room nod in agreement.

> TED STEINBERG
>
> Never again.

CUT TO:

EXT. MAGNUS HQ BUILDING - MORNING
A sprawling metallic high-rise on the outskirts of Beverly Hills like the Nakatomi Plaza of the future.

The mirrored thick glass façade doubles as holographic TV screens portraying different commercials for Magnus products.

SUPER: LOS ANGELES, 2025

INT. MAGNUS HQ BUILDING – CORRIDOR - SAME
DR. HUGH STEPHERN, an eccentric scientist, early 30s, total hermit, walks with DR. GRACE PILARO, early 30s. She's his refined, well-to-do lab partner. At least on the surface.

> GRACE
>
> How come you didn't come to the party last night?

> HUGH
>
> Oh. Um, I had to, I, uh, am moving in to a new place.

> GRACE
>
> Cool. Next party's at your place.

> HUGH
>
> Oh no, Grace, I mean...I don't think...

Grace giggles slightly, turning to Hugh and fake-punching him on the arm.

>   GRACE
> I'm just screwin' with ya, Hugh. Man, you gotta get out
> more.

Hugh blushes slightly as they cross through the -

MAGNUS LOBBY - CONTINUOUS
The place is a massive, very modern room, with polished steel and flawless wood paneling. A futuristic 2-storey sculpture sits in the center.

INT. RESEARCH LAB - MOMENTS LATER
The research lab in the upper floors of Magnus HQ is just as massive as the lobby.

Research staff members are using holographic interfaces to manipulate the design of chemical formulas or using electron microscopes or 3D imaging devices.

Hugh and Grace head to a smaller lab off to a side.

INT. HUGH'S R&D LAB - CONTINUOUS
JOHNNY MYERS, their assistant, late 20s, a wiry, comedic, likeable asshole, reclines against a table, smoking a cigarette. He perks up when they arrive.

>   JOHNNY
> Ah, morning guys.

Johnny fumbles to hide his smoldering cigarette.

>   HUGH
> You mind maybe not smoking around the flammable
> chemicals?

>   JOHNNY
> I like living on the edge.

                    GRACE
Johnny, can you run down and get me a coffee?

                    JOHNNY
Sure. You want anything Hugh?

                    HUGH
No, I'm alright.

                    GRACE
Blended mocha latte, soy milk and foam.

                    JOHNNY
Coffee it is.

Johnny leaves, and Hugh and Grace get to work. Hugh turns on a holographic interface over the table, looks through files.

                    HUGH
Hmm, we finally got the psoriasis compound to stabilize.

                    GRACE
Sweet.

                    HUGH
Actually, not really. The white coats are saying it reeks.

                    GRACE
White coats? What do you think we're wearing?

Hugh looks at his own coat.

> HUGH

Touché.

> (smiles)

Anyway, they want us to put some fragrance on it. Something nice.

> GRACE

And something that won't interfere with the compound.

Hugh opens the fragrance library and scrolls through them.

Johnny returns with the coffees, hands one to Grace and goes to his desk, putting his feet up.

> HUGH

What's better? Flowers or mint?

> GRACE

Mint...no, wait, flowers. White lily, not roses. Guilty men give roses.

From behind Hugh, the door slides open and a man in a business suit and impeccably trimmed hair enters. He is WALTER STEINBERG.

> HUGH

What are they guilty of?

> WALTER STEINBERG

What aren't we guilty of, right buddy?

Walter slaps Hugh on the ass, startling him as he turns around to see Walter. Grace grumbles.

GRACE

You're such an asshole.

WALTER STEINBERG

Good morning to you too, Gracie!
(turns to Hugh)
Just thought I'd pay a visit to my favorite little R&D stud...
(draws out the name)
Huuuuugh.

HUGH
(uncomfortable)
What do you want, Walter?

WALTER STEINBERG

I bring news from the top. The psoriasis project has been scrapped due to budget cuts. I'm sorry.

HUGH

What? Whose call was that?

WALTER STEINBERG

Ms. Walsh and the board. You know how they can be.

HUGH

So what about us?

WALTER STEINBERG

Starting tomorrow, we're putting you three on Dr. Mitchell's team, something about cosmetics. I didn't read the email.

HUGH

Seriously?

WALTER STEINBERG

Don't push it, Hugh. I'm paying you enough, aren't I?

HUGH
(grumbles)

Alright.

WALTER STEINBERG

You always did know your way around a complex chemical formula. Must've gotten that from your uncle.

GRACE

Who's your Uncle?

WALTER STEINBERG

Didn't you know? Hugh here is the nephew of H.G. Golden himself. One of the co-founders of Magnus!

Hugh tries to hide himself from view, totally embarrassed.

HUGH

Walter!

WALTER STEINBERG

Oh come on! You're related to a legend.

JOHNNY

So...what does that make you? Heir to the throne or whatever?

HUGH

If I was, I wouldn't be stuck down here listening to this guy.

WALTER STEINBERG

You know you'd miss me. Okay, I'm off to a board meeting. Probably wanna give me an award or something. Catch you nerds later.

Walter leaves, and Grace heaves a sigh of relief.

JOHNNY
(mock cough)

Cockbite!

Hugh, Grace and Johnny all laugh.

GRACE

I can't believe that guy.

HUGH

He's been the same since college. He's not that bad, really. Once you get through all the layers of douche. He got me the job here.

GRACE

I hate it when he flirts with me. Was he always such a dick?

HUGH

He was a pretty good student, spent time working with the Medic Corps.

JOHNNY

Can we go back to how you're the nephew of Dr. Golden? I mean, hello? You should be running this place by now, not stuck in cosmetics and shit!

HUGH

Eh, I'm just here for the work. I leave the other stuff to Walter.

INT. MAGNUS BOARDROOM - LATER

Walter sits at a long metallic table, looking flustered. Several older gentlemen are gathered around it. A man at the head of the table stares daggers at him.

WALTER STEINBERG

I don't know what you're talking about, Harris.

MR. HARRIS

Your misconduct will cost us more than half our quarterly revenue! And your back-alley deals have made us all look like criminals!

WALTER STEINBERG

Did my father put you up to this? To embarrass me in front of everyone?

MR. HARRIS

Look at this!

He brings up a hologram of the Times news. The cover story is "CORRUPTION AT MAGNUS."

WALTER STEINBERG

Corruption? Seriously? I made this company 8.4 Billion last year with those so-called back alley deals.

>   MR. DONOVAN
> That's not the point, Walter.

>   WALTER STEINBERG
> That is the point! Whatever happened to the ends jus-
> tifying the means?

>   MR. HARRIS
> Only through the proper channels. You've cost us all
> a fortune.

>   WALTER STEINBERG
> I am the senior executive of the company.

>   MR. HARRIS
> Walter, we're filing an injunction against you until we
> get this all sorted out.

Walter sits down, seething.

>   WALTER STEINBERG
> I'll call my father about this.

>   MR. DONOVAN
> Whose idea do you think it was?

INT. HUGH'S NEW HOUSE - NIGHT
Hugh enters the 1950s-style duplex in a fringe suburb of Los Angeles. He recently
inherited this place from his deceased Uncle, whose tastes were as nerdy as his own.

>   HUGH
> Heir to the throne indeed.

An OLD Cocker Spaniel, HERBERT, waddles out to greet him.

HUGH (CONT'D)
Hey Herbie, how you holding' up, old boy?

The whole place has stacks of books and boxes scattered around. There is a display case with preserved animals on a shelf against a wall (birds, cats, and insects). A few horror movie posters on the walls, as well as a shelf full of comic books and anime memorabilia.

There is a virtual reality headset in a corner. Some boxes nearby are marked with Sharpie ink "H.G. Golden."

Hugh clears off a space on a sofa and collapses on it, exhaling deeply.

Grunting, he turns to the boxes, opening one of them. An old Polaroid of H.G. Golden greets him as he opens a box. He sighs as he picks up the picture.

HUGH
Don't worry Uncle Henry, I'll take care of it for ya.

He rummages through the box, pouring over old notebooks, some of which are really faded.

Hugh notices an old handwritten, leather-bound notebook sticking out from the rest. He picks it up and reads it like a great, captivating novel, looking at notes and chemical formulas. He notices some of the dates.

HUGH (CONT'D)
1990? Huh... The legend. Bet you
never saw me becoming a biochemist
too, did you? Yeah, neither did my dad.
(beat)
Speaking of which...

He breaks out a small phone, and calls his dad.

HUGH (CONT'D)
Hey, Dad?

INTERCUT AS NECESSARY WITH -

INT. MORGAN'S LIVING ROOM - NIGHT
MORGAN STEPHERN, 50s, sits in an opulent living room in a large house in the Pacific Palisades.

> MORGAN STEPHERN
>
> Hugh. How's my brother's house? Still living large off of someone else's dime?

> HUGH
>
> No, well, I mean...

> MORGAN STEPHERN
>
> I told you not to call me anymore.

> HUGH
>
> I just thought maybe now we could--

> MORGAN STEPHERN
>
> You still don't get it. Everything you put us through. Years wondering when the phone call was coming? Wondering if you...

> HUGH
>
> Dad, I told you, I've been clean a long time now. Hell, I'm a scientist working for the very company that Uncle H helped build!

> MORGAN STEPHERN
>
> You can give a garbage truck a paint job, it doesn't make it a Maserati. Once a junkie, always a junkie. And now you get my brother's house too. How much more you want to take from me? Huh?

                    HUGH
He wanted me to have this place! Just because you two
didn't get along, don't take it out on me!

            MORGAN STEPHERN (V.O.)
Shut up, you little shit. You didn't earn that place,
you didn't earn anything! You're a loser, always have
been.

                    HUGH
I graduated cum laude from Boston College with a
Master's in biochemistry!

            MORGAN STEPHERN
Oh yeah? Tell that to my degree from Harvard. So
long, kid.

Morgan hangs up on him. Hugh frowns and collapses on the sofa, reading the
journal.

                    HUGH
Jealous prick. I'll earn it. You'll see.

His frown begins to disappear as he gets more engrossed in the book.
    His eyes go wide as he turns a page to see a complex secret formula written
under the headline "Eden."

INSERT – BOOK PAGE –
Words jump out at us like "REVERSING", "AGING PROCESS" and
"CURE."

BACK TO SCENE
Herbert limps over to him. Hugh pets him and reads more of the journal. He
looks at the dog and grins slightly.

INT. HUGH'S NEW HOUSE – THE NEXT NIGHT

He hasn't left. Instead, he's set up a private laboratory in his uncle's study. Hugh mixes chemicals and pours over a holographic laptop.

Hours fall off the clock as he gets increasingly frustrated. His hair is messed up and he almost has a five o'clock shadow.

> HUGH
>
> Come on, this better work...

INT. GRACE'S BEDROOM - NIGHT

Grace is asleep in her bed. A phone on her nightstand rings, which awakens the cat on her bed. She stirs in her silk nightshirt, turns on a lamp and answers the phone.

> GRACE
> (groggy)
>
> Hello?

> HUGH (o.s)
> (excited)
>
> Grace! Are you awake?

> GRACE
>
> It's three in the morning. So, no. Where the hell have you been all day? Walter was pissed.

INTERCUT AS NECESSARY WITH -

INT. HUGH'S HOUSE - NIGHT

> HUGH
>
> Just listen to me, okay? My uncle, he had this diary, right? He was working on something big, I mean really big!

GRACE

What is really big?

HUGH

He created something that could regrow and replicate epidermal tissues!

GRACE (V.O.)

What do you mean? You haven't tested it, have you?

HUGH

Yeah, on my dog!

Grace gets up from her bed, startled.

GRACE

Are you crazy? You experimented on a dog?

HUGH

Look, the dog's twelve years old, he can barely -- never mind! Look, I'll bring you my video log tomorrow. We'll have our own project! We won't have to get stuck with cosmetics!

GRACE

I'll believe you when I see it. Can I go back to sleep now?

HUGH (V.O.)

Fine. Go back to sleep. But the future is NOW.

GRACE

Well, it will still be the future tomorrow. Good night, Hugh.

She hangs up, lost in thought. She tries to get comfortable again as her cat nuzzles her cheek.

INT. HUGH'S R&D LAB - MORNING
Grace walks into the lab. Hugh is already there, getting his video files uploaded into the R&D computer.

> HUGH
>
> Finally, you're here!

> GRACE
>
> Okay, what's this breakthrough you told me about?

> HUGH
>
> The footage speaks for itself. Check it out.

Hugh points at the hologram. It shows an image of his dog, looking very old and sickly.

> GRACE
>
> You did that to your dog?!

> HUGH
>
> He was like that before. Just watch.

The video fast-forwards, showing the dog with progressively less wrinkles on his skin. His skin is tighter, more soft and supple, and he's not limping anymore.

> HUGH (CONT'D)
>
> It only took two hours for that to happen, and that's just
> the first phase. Now look what happens within five hours.

The dog looks like he's reverse-aged at least five years He's healthy and energetic again. Grace can't believe it.

                         GRACE
Holy shit, this is fantastic!

                          HUGH
I know, right?

Grace runs up and kisses him on the cheek. Hugh blushes, taken aback.

                         GRACE
This is incredible! We can save lives with this!

                          HUGH
                (trying to keep his composure)
We can make millions with this!
                        (beat)
And, yeah, the lives thing too. But it needs to be
developed further. We'll need a prototype for human trials.

                         GRACE
How? We need approval from the FDA. And funding.

                          HUGH
We'll go to Steinberg and get his approval. He'll flip
for it. Trust me.

              TED STEINBERG (PRE-LAP)
Absolutely not.

INT. TED STEINBERG'S OFFICE – MAGNUS HQ - LATER
The top-floor office is as opulent as Morgan's living room with classical paint-
ings on the walls. An antique Bible is in a glass case against the wall.

TED, now in his late 80s, but still in great shape, sits at his desk staring across at Hugh and Grace, now crestfallen.

> HUGH
>
> Sir, did you see what it can do? It could change the world! Here, you can read it straight from my Uncle's mouth. He was a former colleague of yours.

> TED STEINBERG
>
> Who?

> HUGH
>
> Dr. Henry Golden. I have his journal here from forty years ago.

Hugh holds out the journal to Ted, who looks in fear, suddenly shocked. Bad memories flood back to him in droves.

> TED STEINBERG
>
> Get that damn thing away from me!

Hugh and Grace are surprised.

> HUGH
>
> Sir?

Ted tries to get his composure back.

> TED STEINBERG
> (exhaling)
> I'm sorry. I knew your uncle, Hugh. He was a good man. But he had some misguided ideas.

HUGH

Sir, just please hear us out.

TED STEINBERG

Son, I understand wanting to carry on your Uncle's legacy. But if it's a grant you want, I'm sorry but I can't approve it.

GRACE

Why not?

TED STEINBERG

One, we could face lawsuits if we use human test subjects without prior analysis. And two, it's not acceptable on moral grounds. You're talking about completely changing everything about the human body, down to the genetic level.

GRACE

Sir, this could be the discovery of a lifetime! Think of the profits!

TED STEINBERG

Now you sound like Ms. Walsh. This is not about money, it's about principles. I'm sorry. Now if you would both excuse me, I have work to get back to, and so do you.

Hugh and Grace get up to leave but not before glancing back at Ted. He looks their way as they exit the room.

EXT. CORDOVA RESTAURANT & BAR - EVENING

Hugh and Grace sit at a table on the patio of the trendy fusion restaurant, having drinks. The candles sitting in glass jars flicker on the table.

> HUGH
>
> I don't get it, why would he turn us down like that?

> GRACE
>
> There's bound to be something else we can do, right?

Hugh takes a swig of wine.

> HUGH
>
> I don't know. It's just, all I've got is my work. I literally have nothing else worth talking about.

> GRACE
>
> Oh, stop. I don't buy that. Come on, tell me something about yourself I don't know.

Hugh groans and lowers his head, taking a sip of his drink.

> HUGH
>
> ...I was born a young bad boy...

> GRACE
>
> Hugh!

> HUGH
>
> Alright, alright. You really want to know something?
> (beat)

I used to be an addict. Your garden variety heroin fiend living on the streets, disappointing his parents.

> GRACE
>
> Shit. I meant like, tell me your favorite movie. But wow.

She smiles, putting him at ease.

                    HUGH
     Dad wasn't an easy man. Drugs took the pain of life
     away.

Hugh rolls up his sleeve, revealing scarred-over syringe marks on his arm. Grace
recoils in shock.

                    HUGH (CONT'D)
     Was a rough few years. But then I cleaned up, moved
     on, studied medicine, and try to make a change.

                    GRACE
     Wow. So bookworm's got some baggage. Who knew?
     For what it's worth, my dad was a dick too. Til he
     walked out... And you *have* made a change. If not in the
     world, then at least in me.

A silent, resonating beat as the two stare at each other.
     It's broken up by the WAITRESS, who brings two more drinks.

                    GRACE
     A toast. To changing. One drink at a time.

                    HUGH
     I'll drink to that.

BEGIN SERIES OF SHOTS –

-    They pour some shots and start downing them.
-    They laugh at each other as they try to toss food into each other's mouths.

- They play a futuristic game of QUARTERS using holographic coins.
- They head to the dance floor, dancing together wildly as a local jazz band plays. The whole place is alive with movement.
- Hugh, drunk, shuts his eyes as he dances with Grace. Grace grabs Hugh's necktie, and pulls him into a kiss! Hugh open his eyes, can't believe it. After a moment of disbelief, he kisses her right back.

EXT. GRACE'S HOUSE - NIGHT

They stumble out of a taxi together, plastered. They trip up the walkway, laughing, to Grace's posh suburban home.

Grace fumbles trying to put her hand on a hand-scanning keypad to unlock the door, finally it opens.

> HUGH
> You know, I should be going home.

> GRACE
> Like hell you are!

She pulls Hugh into the house.

INT. GRACE'S BEDROOM - MORNING

They are both naked but covered by the sheets. They both have bad hangovers. Grace starts to stir.

> GRACE
> Huh? What the...? Where are my clothes?

She rolls over and turns to Hugh, surprised.

> GRACE (CONT'D)
> Hugh? You alive?

                    HUGH
Uhh, what the hell?
                  (panicked)
Oh my God, did we...?!

                    GRACE
                  (smiling)
Ya.

Hugh sits up, wide-eyed and trembling.

                    HUGH
Oh God! What have I done?!

                    GRACE
I wasn't complaining. You were kinda good, actually.

                    HUGH
Well, yeah, but -- oh God, I just slept with my coworker!

Grace laughs while Hugh tries to catch his breath.

                    GRACE
Don't worry about it. I wanted to, okay?

She looks at the clock on the nightstand.

                  GRACE (CONT'D)
Oh crap, we gotta get to work!

INT. HUGH'S R&D LAB - MAGNUS HQ - MORNING
Hugh, Grace and Johnny are all engrossed in their work. Hugh and Grace steal
glances at each other as they try to pretend nothing happened.

Johnny suddenly drops something heavy and it CLANGS loudly on the floor.

Both Hugh and Grace react in pain, clearly still suffering from hangover headaches. Johnny most certainly notices.

> JOHNNY
>
> You guys got drunk? You two actually <u>get</u> drunk?

> HUGH
>
> No, we, um, we didn't...

Johnny totally gets it, and grins deviously.

> JOHNNY
>
> You guys did it, didn't you?

> GRACE
>
> No!

> JOHNNY
>
> You guys totally boned. Did the ol' beaker squeaker. The scientific pull-out method. Banged like lab rats--

Hugh turns a shade of purple as an exec stares at them from across the room.

> HUGH
>
> Oh for Christ's sake... Ted said no to Eden!

Johnny is instantly snapped out of his joking mood.

> JOHNNY
>
> Wait, what?

GRACE

He nixed the idea. We're done.

JOHNNY

Corporations, man. Some bullshit.

Hugh smiles, but then it fades away.

HUGH

If only we could find some funding.

GRACE

Well, unless you know someone with a spare forty mill laying around.

Johnny cuts in promptly.

JOHNNY

I do!

HUGH

Bullshit, you do not.

JOHNNY

I have an aunt who works here. She's one of the higher-ups.

GRACE PILARO

How high up?

JOHNNY

She's in charge of development and public relations.

GRACE
Your aunt is Katherine Walsh?! You've gotta be kidding!

JOHNNY
How do you think I still have this job? Nepotism is the shit.

HUGH
Do you think she'll approve this?

JOHNNY
Totally. Give her enough incentive and she'll go for it.

GRACE
A de-aging formula worth billions should be enough incentive.

JOHNNY
I'll give her a call and we can set something up.
(smiles)
So... Is your little sexperiment over?

INT. KATHERINE'S MANSION - lIVING ROOM - AFTERNOON
Hugh and Grace sit in a mansion that could house a small country. High-tech everything. Marble everything else.
    Johnny reclines on a sofa. Grace looks around the room enviously.

HUGH
No wonder you never worry about money.

JOHNNY
Yeah, it's a good life. Here she comes.

KATHERINE WALSH drives up in her driveway in a futuristic hybrid Ferrari. A socialite and corporate black widow, she's still very attractive in her 40s.
   Katherine enters the room.

                    KATHERINE WALSH
          Hey Johnny.

Katherine embraces Johnny, then turns to Hugh and Grace.

                    KATHERINE WALSH (CONT'D)
          You must be Doctors Stephern and Pilaro. My Johnny's
          told me about you.

She shakes hands with Hugh and Grace.

                    KATHERINE WALSH (CONT'D)
          Heard you two have something "revolutionary" to
          show me.

                    GRACE
          Yes ma'am. We've had a breakthrough on an experi-
          mental formula, one that could reverse aging.

Katherine takes a seat in a plush armchair, putting her feet on an ottoman.

                    KATHERINE WALSH
          How so?

                    HUGH
          Basically it's a regenerative reagent. You see, when a
          person gets old they start to lose certain proteins in the
          skin layers. The chemical compound corrects that by
          re-stimulating production, manipulating ribo-nucleic
          acids and-

KATHERINE WALSH

Kid, do I look like a scientist to you? Seriously.

HUGH

Uh, well... it stops aging and makes people young again.

KATHERINE WALSH

Does it make people just look younger than they really are?

HUGH

Better, it actually rebuilds the body. It could add years onto your life. Take a look at this.

Hugh brings up his portable computer, showing the original clinical trial with his dog. Katherine watches, astonished.

KATHERINE WALSH

Have you shown this to anyone else?

GRACE

Just to Ted a few days ago. He turned us down. Moral grounds, he said.

KATHERINE WALSH

Everyone will want to feel younger, or just be younger! This could be a gold mine! You'd think Teddy of all people would be drooling over something like this.

HUGH

Yeah, it doesn't make sense.

KATHERINE WALSH

The formula works, right?

                    HUGH
On my dog, at least.

                KATHERINE WALSH
Let me worry about Ted. You two work on a prototype.
I'll give you the space, the manpower, the equipment,
everything. Think forty million will help you get there?

Hugh is dumbstruck, and Grace is smiling. Johnny gets up from the sofa and stands next to her.

                    JOHNNY
What did I tell you? I knew she'd love it!

Katherine kisses Johnny on the forehead.

                KATHERINE WALSH
                   (laughing)
It's about time helping you paid off.

A wicked grin on Johnny's face as he uncorks champagne.

                KATHERINE WALSH
Now let's have a drink. You two have a lot of work to
do.

They toast, and drink the champagne.

INT. ELYSIUM LABS - MAGNUS RESEARCH FACILITY - DAY
The massive, ultra-high tech cluster of rooms is humming with activity. Katherine leads Hugh and Grace right into the middle of the room, where scientists busy themselves with large-scale holographs, mixing compounds and running simulations on the variations of Hugh's formula.

For Hugh, it's like walking into his own Jurassic Park.

KATHERINE WALSH

Welcome to Elysium! Our own private heaven inside
of the Magnus Universe. Quite the step up from your
little R&D labs, huh?

HUGH

My God, it's incredible!

Johnny runs up to the three from across the room. He's dressed in a slick, three-
piece suit.

JOHNNY

This is where the magic happens!

HUGH

I am sorry for everything I've ever said about you.

JOHNNY

Thanks, buddy – wait, what did you say?

Changing the topic --

GRACE

So Johnny, what do you do here?

JOHNNY

I'm your new liaison with Elysium Biotech, a subsid-
iary of Magnus Corporation, for Ms. Walsh.

GRACE

Why so proper? She's your aunt.

JOHNNY

Shh! Not in front of the science guys!

They all laugh, and Johnny blushes.

KATHERINE WALSH
(clapping hands)
Alright people, let's change the world!

INT. ELYSIUM labs - MAGNUS RESEARCH FACILITY - DAY

SUPER: "6 MONTHS LATER"
Hugh brings a vial of the new-and-improved Eden formula into a room with tables, gurneys and kennels. Some scientists are on hand to observe.
    Grace, Johnny and Walter arrive as well.

GRACE

Do you know what's going on?

JOHNNY

No idea.

Hugh dons a lab coat and some large goggles, grinning like a mad scientist. The entire room has cameras that are recording the entire test.

HUGH

Dr. Hugh Stephern. Day is September 14, 2025, at seven-thirty PM. First test of Eden Formula, version 1.2.045. Subject is a common brown monkey, adult female, about nine years old, showing signs of advanced aging. Lots of wrinkles, fur is mostly shed, spots on the skin, and discoloration of the eyes and tongue. Administering five ccs of the formula reagent.

He puts on his goggles and picks up the syringe.

> HUGH (CONT'D)
>
> Brace yourselves!

Hugh looks around at the scientists observing.

> HUGH (CONT'D)
>
> What? I've always wanted to say that.

He delivers the dose to the monkey. She hollers a bit when the syringe goes in, but the screaming stops.

> HUGH (CONT'D)
>
> Vitals?

> SCIENTIST #1
>
> Heart rate, blood pressure and cellular activity are stable.

> HUGH
>
> Good.

The monkey begins to react. Its eyes become clearer, its fur looks stronger and sleeker. It begins to de-age. Everyone is awestruck.

Moments later, however, the monkey starts to convulse on the gurney. Scientist #1 lays tries to calm her down.

The monkey flails, breaking from the straps as its body begins to mutate. The new Fur is falling out, revealing red and pulpy flesh and bulging veins.

The monkey grabs Scientist #1 and bites him on the arm. Blood spurts from the gash. Scientist #1 HOWLS in pain, mimicked by the furious primate.

> HUGH
>
> Jesus Christ. Everyone out. Go!

The mutated monkey skitters off the gurney and charges for a nearby victim.

                    SCIENTIST #2
          Tranq her! Tranq her!

The staff runs for the exits, including Hugh and Grace. Another scientist readies a dart gun with a tranquilizer. He takes aim but accidentally shoots a fleeing scientist, who falls.

                SCIENTIST WITH DART
          Damn!

He readies another round as the mutated monkey approaches. Blood is dripping from its open jaws, and it lunges. He makes the shot right in its chest, and the monkey slows down slightly. Another shot, and the monkey drops.

            SCIENTIST WITH DART (CONT'D)
          It's alright! She's down!

Everyone slowly comes back into the room, looking at the body of the monkey. Hugh kneels over the monkey's body with a syringe.

                      HUGH
          Is she out?

                SCIENTIST WITH DART
          Yes, Doc.

Hugh takes a sample of blood. The body convulses again and everyone steps back in terror. The scientist shoots two more darts. The monkey is now well and truly dead.
      Grace assists the wounded scientist.

GRACE PILARO

Get the medic in here, now!

The bitten scientist cradles his bleeding arm. He is led out of the room by some other scientists. Off to a side, Walter is scowling.

INT. ELYSIUM - TESTING ROOM - DAY
SUPER: 3 Weeks Later

Katherine, Johnny and a few SCIENTISTS stand by a large holograph screen portraying a video conference call with Ted, Walter and several other Magnus Board Members and investors.

Hugh stands off in a corner with Grace, speaking privately and sweating bullets. He hasn't shaved in a while.

HUGH

What if it happens again? I still have nightmares about
that damn monkey.

GRACE

It's going to work, don't worry.

We fixed the strain, found the missing sequence. FDA
signed off.

HUGH

This is our last shot.

GRACE

We've come a long way. You got this.

JOHNNY

Come on, man. It'll be alright.

Hugh hugs them both, then walks to the center of the room.

An old man, JOSEPH RICHARDS, is strapped to a gurney near a table with a vial of the formula. Hugh clears his throat.

> HUGH
>
> Ladies and gentlemen, my name is Dr. Hugh Stephern, and what follows is a test of the Eden Formula, version 1.8.946. It's been a long road, but previous recent animal tests showed substantial positive changes in physical appearance. Now we will administer the formula to our first human test subject. Joseph Richards. Adult male, African American, age seventy-four, history of heart disease.

He turns to Joseph on the gurney.

> HUGH (CONT'D)
>
> How are you feeling Mr. Richards?

> JOSEPH RICHARDS
>
> Like a very nervous lab rat?

> HUGH
>
> Don't worry sir, this should only take a few minutes. Okay, if everyone's ready, I will now administer the Eden agent directly into his bloodstream.

He administers the dose to Joseph, who shuts his eyes tightly in anticipation. Hugh takes the needle out. Everyone in the room and on the monitors watch closely.

TED STEINBERG
(under his breath)
Here we go again...

HUGH
Sir, do you feel any different?

JOSEPH RICHARDS
Nothing.

A bio-scan shows his heart rate and nerve conduction activity. Joseph starts to tremble slightly.

JOSEPH RICHARDS (CONT'D)
Wait... I feel something...

The bio-scan shows an elevated heart rate, and Joseph starts going into convulsions on the gurney.

GRACE
He's having a heart attack! Get him out of there!

The staff panics and tries to unstrap Joseph from the gurney, but Hugh pushes them away.

HUGH
No! Wait!

Everyone watches on in suspense. Gradually, Joseph stops quaking, and his heart rate goes back to normal. He is still breathing heavily, as if he just got off a roller coaster.

HUGH (CONT'D)
Mr. Richards, what happened? How are you feeling now?

JOSEPH RICHARDS
I... I... it tingles.

HUGH
It's okay, that's normal. That's the formula reacting with the proteins in your body.

The monitor shows Joseph's face and arms, where most of the aging symptoms are. There are wrinkles, sagging skin folds and some discolored spots.

Gradually, they begin to fade away. The skin gets reattached to the muscles, reducing the appearances of the wrinkles, the saggy folds tighten up, and the spots disappear. His hair also regains its color and his eyes become brighter.

JOSEPH RICHARDS
What's going on? I feel -- sharper.

TED STEINBERG
(on video screen, to himself)
Son of a bitch finally did it.

The bio-scan shows he has de-aged by 15 years. His bone and muscle density, heart rate, nerve activity and vital signs all improve.

With an encouraging nod from Grace, Hugh unstraps him from the gurney. Joseph gets up, slowly, getting used to his new body. He looks at his own hands and arms, and touches his face and hair.

JOSEPH RICHARDS (CONT'D)
Mirror. Can I have a mirror please?

A scientist hands him a small mirror, and he looks at his own face with a look of wonder. He caresses his own face, noticing the wrinkles are gone.

JOSEPH RICHARDS (CONT'D)
(astonished)

My God... I must be dreaming!

HUGH

I assure you, it is very much real.

Joseph keeps looking in the mirror.

JOSEPH RICHARDS

Martha... she won't recognize me when I come home. I am SMOKIN!

(a beat)

My God, it's a miracle!

HUGH

No. It's science.

Joseph has a slow smile come to his face, and trembles in awe. A single tear falls from his eye. He runs up to Hugh and hugs him tightly.

JOSEPH RICHARDS

Thank you... Thank you!

Everyone is in total disbelief, everyone in the room and watching via video. One of the investors in a group of video screens shakes his head in disbelief.

CARL

It's a fake! You wasted our time with this stunt, Doctor?

KATHERINE

Carl, what are you talking about? Did you see what that man went through?

CARL

It's a trick! Anyone could've pulled that off!

Joseph walks up to one of the video cameras and shoves his face into it.

JOSEPH RICHARDS

You see this?!

He shows off his face to the camera.

JOSEPH RICHARDS (CONT'D)

Do you see this? I'm younger! I got more years with my Martha! It really works!

CARL hangs up the video call in a huff. All the other investors stay on the call, whispering among themselves.

TERRY

The rest of us are convinced. We'd like to thank Dr. Stephern, Dr. Pilaro and all the research staff, including Ms. Walsh for inviting us to this most impressive presentation.

KATHERINE WALSH

So gentlemen, have we got a deal?

TERRY

Yes, Ms. Walsh. We have a deal. Congratulations.

Everyone applauds. Hugh prays quietly, holding his head up.

> HUGH
> (whispering)
>
> Thank you.

Grace embraces Johnny, ecstatic.

Ted, on the video call, does not share in the celebration, but instead hangs up. Walter watches on, a twinge of envy.

INT. DUPONT HOTEL (HOLLYWOOD) - EVENING

Magnus Corp is hosting a black-tie gala for the release of the Eden Formula at the five-star facility.

A DJ plays upbeat electronic music. Along the walls, there are video screens showing promotional footage, with beautiful men and women, slogans such as "Rejuvenative," "Return to Youth," "Take a Trip to Eden" and the Magnus and Eden logos.

Grace, in a body-hugging exquisite gown, joins Hugh at a table, bringing some wine glasses.

> GRACE
>
> Hugh, why are you sitting alone?

Hugh says nothing.

> GRACE (CONT'D)
>
> Come on Hugh, this whole party is for us, and for our discovery! Okay, well, mostly your discovery.

> HUGH
>
> Nah, it's not just me. It's for everyone.

GRACE

So why are you sitting alone?

HUGH

I invited my father here tonight. He didn't come.

GRACE

I'm sorry. He tell you why?

HUGH

Even after all this, he still hates me. His own son makes a discovery that can change the world, and he still thinks I'm a loser!

Hugh pounds the table.

Grace tries to calm him down.

GRACE

At some point, Hugh, changing the world forever is going to have to be enough for you.

She lifts up his face and smiles at him.

HUGH

Yeah, you're right.

Grace kisses him on the lips.

GRACE

Now, let's go have fun because I did not wear this dress for nothing.

Hugh smiles. Grace leads Hugh through the party. They find Johnny flirting with some women and drinking. Johnny cheers when he sees Hugh and Grace.

JOHNNY
Hugh! Grace! Get over here!

They come up to him. Clearly, Johnny is more than tipsy.

JOHNNY (CONT'D)
These two here are the best scientists in the history of planet Earth!

The women around him laugh, and Grace takes a step back.

HUGH
He's smashed.

JOHNNY
Nuh-uh, I'm totally fine! See?

Johnny tries walking a straight line while putting his fingers to his nose and some of the girls help him.
When he regains his balance, he comes face-to-face with Ted Steinberg, who smiles at the scene.

TED STEINBERG
I think someone's had too much.

Johnny desperately tries to regain composure. Ted turns to Hugh and Grace. Katherine comes by with a champagne glass.

TED STEINBERG (CONT'D)
Dr. Stephern, Dr. Pilaro, you've made a great contribution to science. And to Magnus. If your uncle was here now, he'd be real proud.

Hugh blushes as Grace and Katherine pat him on the back.
Walter stands off to a side, not looking very comfortable around everyone. He musters up some courage and cuts in.

WALTER STEINBERG
And it was through <u>my</u> contacts that we got the distribution deals. You create 'em, I'll sell 'em! It's a hell of a team.

Ted is really annoyed, and brings him off to a side. Hugh and the team continue to party in the background.

TED STEINBERG
Walter, a word with you please?

Ted and Walter walk to the bar.

WALTER STEINBERG
Dad? What's going on?

TED STEINBERG
Walter, I've given this a lot of thought.

WALTER STEINBERG
What?

TED STEINBERG

We have a revolutionary product on our hands and we need to make sure nothing distracts from that. Not in the press, not on Wall Street, not in the boardroom. The board has decided that Katherine will succeed me in running Magnus, with Hugh and Grace operating R&D.

WALTER STEINBERG

What about my commission?

TED STEINBERG

You'll have your commission, but you will remain as vice president. With your recent exploits and the whole audit, we feel this is in the best interest for the company.

WALTER STEINBERG

So... that's the way it is?

TED STEINBERG

Perhaps this will teach you some humility. Now if you'll excuse me, I need to talk to some investors.

Ted gets up to go, but Walter grabs his arm.

TED STEINBERG (CONT'D)

Let go. Now.

Walter gives him a dark stare, and reluctantly lets go. Ted walks away. Walter is furious, and goes back to the party to look for Katherine. He pushes through some chatting folks and finds her on the dance floor.

KATHERINE WALSH
(smiling deviously)
Hey! You want to dance?

WALTER STEINBERG
We need to talk, now.

She smiles wickedly, thinking maybe she knows what's going on with him. He pulls her off to a side at a small private table in the corner of the room.

KATHERINE WALSH
What's the problem? You seem upset.

WALTER STEINBERG
Did you know you're getting promoted?

It's news to her. She laughs with delight.

KATHERINE WALSH
Thanks for telling me!

WALTER STEINBERG
(about to lose it)
After everything I did for the company? All the deals, all the contacts, and you're getting promoted over me?!

KATHERINE WALSH
Well, I'm not the one who got the company in trouble with those deals under the table.

WALTER STEINBERG

Who cares about that?! You and your friends owe everything to me!

KATHERINE WALSH

Just because you're the founder's son, you think that makes you entitled to something? You're not as special as you think, Walter.

WALTER STEINBERG

You spiteful cunt!

KATHERINE WALSH

My point exactly.

Walter storms away without a word, while Katherine smiles, triumphant. Walter shoves aside a photographer near the entrance to the room on his way out.

PHOTOGRAPHER

Asshole.

The crowd around the door swells, and lots of flashbulbs go off. Into the party walks a beautiful woman, actress SHAUNA BECKETT.
    She heads into the middle of the room and gets a microphone.

SHAUNA BECKETT

How's everyone doing tonight?

The crowd cheers.

SHAUNA BECKETT (CONT'D)

You know, as an actress, I use cosmetics all the time. But when I heard about the new Eden Formula, I couldn't believe it! I mean, a little injection that could stop me from aging? It's almost too good to be true! But I've seen what it can do, and I am in! In fact, I'll be one of its new spokespeople so get used to seeing even more of this face – but younger.

More cheering.

SHAUNA BECKETT (CONT'D)

And don't forget to catch my latest movie, "Remain Silent" November first. Thanks everyone, enjoy!

C
U
T

T
O
:

ON A TV – THE EDEN COMMERCIAL

EXT. JUNGLE SET –

An old woman searches through the jungle wilderness until she comes to a clearing with a large majestic, sparkling fountain. As she approaches, she spies a decorative silver platter laying on a rock holding a small sleek syringe with EDEN written on it.

She looks at the fountain, then takes the syringe and injects herself with it. She shows her left hand, which at first is wrinkly, becoming slender and youthful again. Her face becomes more graceful and youthful as well. It's a magical transformation before our eyes.

SPOKESMODEL (V.O.)
Everything old is new again. Regenerate. Rejuvenate.
EDEN.

Superimpose Eden logo and slogan: "Live Your Life, Younger!"

PULL BACK to reveal we're in -

INT. WALTER'S PENTHOUSE - EVENING
Walter, scotch in hand, watches the commercial in disgust. The commercial ends
and a NEWS REPORT begins.

ON TV –

NEWS ANCHOR
The first shipments of new youth serum wonder-drug
Eden have been sent out across the country, with more
on the way. Promising to add years to your life, Magnus
spokesperson Katherine Walsh said they can barely
keep up with the demand that—

CLICK.
Walter turns the TV off with a dirty scowl.

A couple of days have passed since the party. Walter keeps drinking as he
walks over and stares out at a 180 degree panoramic view of LA.

The twinkling lights of Hollywood, the multiple cell towers pinging, new
freeways, and more holographic billboards than you could count.

Quite a few of those billboards run ads for Eden. Others show clips with
Hugh and Grace's faces – the creators of youth and new life! Walter downs his
whiskey. He's drunk, spouting off to the general masses below.

WALTER STEINBERG

Sure. We turn our backs on war and carnage, but can't possibly look the other way on wrinkles... Liars, backstabbers and superficial narcissists thinking they are part of saving the world. You're just delaying the inevitable for profit.

You think I went too far, dad? Don't trust me?? Where would you be without all that money I made you? Huh? You have to do whatever it takes! Pass me up? For Huuuugh?

You want to create Eden? You want to change the face of the world? We can do that. Yes... we can do that.

Walter looks out the window, seeing his reflection among the city skyline. An evil grin slides across his face.

INT. SHAUNA BECKETT'S LIMO - EVENING

Shauna sits in the back seat of a limo, wearing a flowing gown. She snorts a small line of coke off a pocket mirror. She also grabs a small syringe of Eden and shoots up with it. She can feel the formula coursing through her, making her beautiful.

SHAUNA BECKETT

Fuck me, this is heaven!

Shauna smiles at the crowds of paparazzi outside her limo. She opens a small compartment in an armrest looking for another syringe of Eden, but they are all empty. She fumbles around frantically looking for a fresh one.

SHAUNA BECKETT (CONT'D)

Shit! Shit, where is it? Gotcha!

She finds a fresh one, and quickly injects herself with it. She sighs, happy, and preps herself for her fans as she exits the limo looking 10 years younger.

BEGIN MONTAGE – EDEN SPREADS LIKE WILDFIRE OVER 6 MONTHS

- Stores featuring signs for EDEN have lines around the
- block.
- Plastic Surgeons give patients Eden injections like Botox.
- Women have Eden parties, injecting each other with youth.
- More commercials for Eden boasting its successes.
- Newspaper and TV reports about how it has become the most widely used drug since Penicillin and how Magnus stock
- prices have sky-rocketed.
- Hugh and Grace are guests of honor at galas and events all over the country. Hugh getting a bit more comfortable with his new life.
- Everyone walking around seems younger, stronger, healthier.
- Stores have SOLD OUT OF EDEN signs.
- Crowds of people scream at store fronts that are out of the product and fight over last remaining doses across the country.

END MONTAGE

EXT. DOWNTOWN LOS ANGELES SHOPPING CENTER - DAY
SUPER: 6 MONTHS AFTER LAUNCH

A group of men and women line up outside a posh downtown store waiting for the new supply of Eden to come in. It's like being outside Best Buy on Thanksgiving.

They all seem to be jonesing just a little bit, checking themselves and preening in mirrors and holographic IPhones.

At the end of the line, an OLDER WOMAN covered by a shawl, sunglasses and housecoat starts to shake as she waits.

As she trembles, she can't take it anymore and she starts to make her way to the front of the line. As other people in line start to (ad lib) YELL at her, one grabs the shawl off of her.

She swings around to the person responsible and we can see her skin has become a red, pulpy irritated mess and her veins are bulging. She emits a guttural growl and ATTACKS as we –

SMASH CUT TO:

INT. ELYSIUM – RESEARCH LAB – DAY
Hugh BURTS into the lab breathing really heavily. He looks very pale and haggard, ready to collapse. Dozens of scientists and employees crowd try to approach him with questions or for approval.

> HUGH
>
> Get out of my way!

He shoves some scientists away to get to a coffee dispenser. It's empty.

> HUGH (CONT'D)
>
> Fuck! Where's the coffee?! Who's the asshole who didn't make new coffee?

Grace and Johnny come in and see Hugh acting like this.

> GRACE
>
> Hugh, baby, you need to relax.

> HUGH
>
> You relax! I haven't slept in four days! Katherine's breathing down my neck! It's just... I can't take anymore!

johnny

Can't take what?

HUGH

Ever since Eden took off, we've been under the gun to create more supply. 24/7. We can't keep up anymore. And new products! Curing aging wasn't enough. We have to cure ALL problems? I'm not GOD!

JOHNNY

Goes with the golden goose territory, man.

HUGH

Shut up, Johnny!

JOHNNY

Hey, I'm not your assistant anymore Doctor Stephern.

Hugh growls angrily, and Grace puts a hand on his shoulder.

GRACE

Hugh?

HUGH

Leave me the fuck alone!

Hugh shoves her. Grace is so shocked that she runs out of the room crying. Johnny is dumbfounded. Hugh realized what he just did, and runs out of the room to follow her.

INT. ELYSIUM - HALLWAY - CONTINUOUS
Hugh catches up with Grace, who is looking clearly distraught.

HUGH

Grace!

Grace slaps Hugh across the face.

GRACE

Bastard!

Hugh pauses, then looks right at her.

HUGH

Baby, I'm sorry. It's just... I think I'm gonna crack.

GRACE

You just did.

HUGH

Look, I don't want us to fight. It's just, nothing's simple anymore.

GRACE

I know. It's the success of Eden. We had no idea what we were really getting into.

Hugh exhales, then slouches against the wall. Grace puts her hands on his shoulders. She feels sorry for him. After all, she loves him.

GRACE (CONT'D)

I just want you – us - to be happy, alright? That's all.

HUGH

(eyes down)

I know, but I don't have time.

                    GRACE
        Maybe I could call up Katherine, get you a vacation.
        You need it.

Johnny pokes his head out of the break room.

                    JOHNNY
        Uh, guys? I think you should see this!

                    HUGH
        What?

                    JOHNNY
        Just get in here!

INT. ELYSIUM - RESEARCH LAB - MOMENTS LATER
Hugh and Grace come in. Johnny points up at the TV.

                 NEWS ANCHOR #2
        This is Craig Anderson at GNN with some breaking
        news in downtown Los Angeles, where we've gotten
        reports a creature of some sort is on a bloody rampage
        and many have been left dead. We have some amateur
        video coming in now from the scene. Please be advised
        this footage is live and extremely graphic.

INSERT – Streaming iPhone Video -
A bloody massacre as something with oozing, pulpy skin and bulging veins attacks people, ripping throats apart. Blood shoots up like fountains.

BACK TO SCENE -
Hugh and Company watch, at first confused, then horrified.

Hugh almost gags at the sight. Grace is speechless.

                         HUGH
          What the hell is that?

The TV cuts back to the inside of the news studio. Craig is in shock too.

                    CRAIG ANDERSOn
          Jesus.

The reporter gets an update.

                    CRAIG ANDERSON (CONT'D)
          Um, we just received an update. We're getting new
          reports of other similar attacks in Chicago, in Times
          Square in New York and an apartment complex in
          Miami. We don't have a death toll for you yet, but many
          are feared dead. We have some News Copter footage of
          the Miami situation.

The TV cuts to helicopter footage - a few buildings are on fire, and there are a hand-
ful of hideous, ravenous figures in the streets, tearing apart anyone they can find.
     POLICE open fire and shoot these monsters, killing them on live television.

                    CRAIG ANDERSON (V.O.) (CONT'D)
          Oh my. I apologize for... What? Reports now, creatures
          have been sighted in at least ten major cities. We've
          never seen anything like this! God help the victims
          and please, if you're in the immediate area, stay off the
          streets!

BACK TO SCENE - Hugh and the others in the lab.

HUGH

What are those things?

JOHNNY

You ever watch horror movies?

GRACE

You're not serious...?

JOHNNY

Damn right. We got mothafucking zombies up in here!

HUGH

That's impossible!

GRACE

Wait, shut up! What did he just say?

ON TV –
Back in the news studio.

CRAIG ANDERSON

We've just received word from the CDC, Center for Disease Control. Samples from two of these creatures have been found to contain an unknown toxin in their blood- streams. No further explanation has been given. Let's go over to my colleague Sharon Baldwin who has more information.

SHARON, a wrinkle-free blonde woman with very young, tight skin, is going into convulsions at her news desk. She starts to foam at the mouth and her skin starts turning blood-red.

CRAIG ANDERSON (V.O.) (CONT'D)
Sharon! Somebody get a doctor!

Sharon starts screaming in delirium and agony. She reaches into a handbag looking for a vial of Eden, but they are empty.

Her skin starts pulsating and veins start bulging. As Craig gets closer, she turns on him, ripping his face apart with her bare hands. The screaming is blood-curdling.

The TV cuts to COLOR BARS and then a graphic that says "WE ARE EXPERIENCING TECHNICAL DIFFICULTIES."

BACK TO SCENE – ELYSIUM LAB
Johnny starts changing channels, most have turned to Color Bars until we reach E! Entertainment TV.

E! News is covering a red carpet event. We can see Shauna Beckett making her way across the screen.

REPORTER (O.S)
Shauna! Shauna! We're live on E!

With that, Shauna turns to the camera, heaves, and pukes up a torrent of blood. Her skin begin to boil and veins bulge as she turns into a zombie and ATTACKS the Reporter.

BACK TO SCENE –

HUGH
What the fuck just happened?

JOHNNY
Our spokesperson just ate someone's face on live TV. This isn't good.

They change the channel again -

MARK ELLIS (V.O.)
This is Mark Ellis with Fox News. Riot police have
been dispatched all over the Los Angeles area to contain the threat. The National Guard is being mobilized,
and people are being urged to stay in their homes and
keep all doors and windows locked.

Johnny looks at Grace and Hugh, stunned. Everyone else in the room is just as
terrified.

HUGH
Oh God!

GRACE
Hugh?

Hugh points at the screen.

HUGH
Tell me they didn't look like the monkey from the first
test.

A sudden realization hits her. It <u>does</u> look like the monkey. The TV cuts to the
Emergency Broadcast System, with a blaring alert sound. They shut it off.

GRACE
No way!...That's impossible!

JOHNNY
What, you think Eden did this to people?

HUGH
(starting to panic)
No, it's a coincidence! It couldn't have caused that!
Could it?

JOHNNY
Look, we don't know anything. Maybe it's something
else! Poisoned water supply. Mad cow disease. The
Lakers lost another game.

HUGH
It's everywhere. We need to stop all shipments, start a
recall and hold a press conference. Get me Ted!

INT. MAGNUS CONFERENCE ROOM – THE NEXT MORNING
Ted Steinberg holds an emergency press conference, standing behind a podium in front of a slew of reporters. He keeps his calm demeanor. Off to the side
stand Katherine, Hugh, Grace, and other executives. Security is also present.

TED STEINBERG
Ladies and Gentlemen, thank you all for coming. Due
to recent horrific events and much speculation, I've
called this conference to explain the Eden Formula.

REPORTER #1
Is Eden responsible for the dozens of grisly murders
that continue to take place?

TED STEINBERG
Eden was given approval by the FDA prior to manufacturing. We have provided data on all our clinical
trials, and we have demonstrated that the product is
safe.

We strive to achieve perfection in every facet of our business, but as such we must be held to an even higher standard and make sure we are ever-vigilant. So regretfully we are announcing that as of today, we --

A MAN in the middle of the crowd suddenly stands up and aims a handgun at Ted. The rest plays out in slow motion.

POP! POP!

Hugh jumps in front of Grace, falling on top of her, covering her as blood splatters across his white coat.

Ted falls to the floor, clutching two gunshot wounds to his chest. Panic ensues as reporters and executives flee for the exit.

Security draws their weapons and opens fire on the hitman, peppering him with bullets. They then grab Ted and carry him into a secret door behind the conference room.

Katherine is frozen in fear as SIRENS ring out in the distance. The sirens fade into a PHONE RINGING (O.S.)

INT. WALTER'S PENTHOUSE - MORNING

Walter is on a sofa getting high (not on Eden) and looking totally out of it. He's been on a drug binge for a few days, knowing what's been happening.

His phone RINGS in the B.G.

ANNIE, blonde, mid-30s, walks out of the bathroom. She quickly does a line.

> ANNIE
>
> Babe! You gonna get that or what?

Walter grumbles and reaches for the phone.

> WALTER STEINBERG
> (out of it)
>
> Steinberg.

MR. HARRIS (V.O.)
Walter, I take it you've heard?

WALTER STEINBERG
Heard what? Who is this?

INT. MAGNUS BOARDROOM - MORNING
Several executives sit at the table, all looking nervous and sad. A couple women cry. MR. HARRIS and MR. DONOVAN (from the first board room scene) are among them.

MR. HARRIS
It's Harris. I'm here with the other Board Members. Where *you* should be.

WALTER STEINBERG (O.S)
Sorry, Harris, but it was made real clear I wasn't wanted. So whatever favor you need, you can shove--

MR. HARRIS
Son, your father has been shot.

Beat.

WALTER STEINBERG (O.S.)
<u>What?!</u>

MR. HARRIS
He was shot during the press conference this morning. And we can't find Ms. Walsh. The board has agreed to transfer control of the company to you. You are now the CEO of Magnus Pharmaceuticals.

INT. WALTER'S PENTHOUSE - SAME

> WALTER STEINBERG
> What? When did... Why wasn't I told about this?

> MR. HARRIS (O.S.)
> I'm telling you now. We need your help to fix this mess.

> WALTER STEINBERG
> What mess?

> MR. HARRIS (V.O.)
> The CDC approached us about the attacks. They found that all of the creatures had Eden in their bloodstreams. A full investigation is pending. Your father was about to announce a stop to production and recall of Eden when he was--

> WALTER STEINBERG
> Fuck the CDC. That doesn't prove anything. I'll handle them. In the meantime, I want the production of Eden accelerated.

Annie lounges on the floor snorting more cocaine while the conversation is going on. She looks at Walter nonchalantly.

> MR. HARRIS (V.O.)
> Walter, are you sure? What if--

> WALTER STEINBERG
> There's no problem with the formula!

> MR. HARRIS (V.O.)
> You'd better be right about that!

WALTER STEINBERG

Alert the procurement team – anyone still alive – have 'em start rounding up those fuckers. And send the chopper asap. I'm coming in.

Walter hangs up and collapses on the sofa. He snorts one more quick line.

ANNIE

What did they want?

WALTER STEINBERG

My father's dead. I'm the new CEO of Magnus. It's finally happened.

ANNIE

You okay?

WALTER STEINBERG

I didn't know it would be like this... I gotta do damage control. Make sure everything stays on track. Make sure no one... Shit!

Realizing something, he picks up his phone and dials.

ANNIE

On track for what? Walt?

WALTER STEINBERG
(into phone)

It's Steinberg. I need you to meet me at Magnus in 90 minutes... I don't care what your mission calls for. You meet me there or your only mission will be scraping buckets of flesh off the sidewalk.

He hangs up. Walter's in his own slightly coked-out head, thinking.

ANNIE

Baby, what's going on?

WALTER STEINBERG

Huh? Nothing. Annie, you aren't going to say a word about anything. You are gonna stay here and keep your mouth shut, and when I get back I'll make sure you've got enough Eden to make you look like a child pageant star the rest of your life.

ANNIE

Aw baby, you are gonna spoil me.

WALTER STEINBERG

You have no idea.

Annie sexy crawls over to Walter, feeling really turned on and moaning pleasurably. Annie rips Walter's shirt open, and Walter returns the favor as they start making out.

WALTER STEINBERG

Baby, my father just died and I've got a chopper to catch in 10 minutes.

ANNIE

So...Just a blow job then?

Walter smiles.

INT. ELYSIUM RESEARCH LAB - MORNING
Grace is still in shock, panicking and unable to speak. Hugh holds her close for comfort. She resists.

HUGH

Grace... Grace! Calm down!

GRACE

Hugh, you saw what just happened! Ted just-- He--

Hugh grabs Grace's shoulders.

HUGH

Look, we'll just wait here, okay? It'll be alright.

Johnny bursts in, startling the two.

JOHNNY MYERS

We need to go! Look!

Johnny turns on the TV and the news feeds are back. There are cops and National Guard battling ZOMBIES everywhere, including right outside the building.

Other scientists scurry through the halls behind them, including DR. WYNN.

DR. WYNN

Hugh, guys, come on! We need to get up top.

JOHNNY

Is the company chopper still on the roof?

DR. WYNN

They already took it. But we need to get to the higher
levels and stay there. They're right outside!

Dr. Wynn and the other scientists leave. The news report on TV is still going on.

NEWS REPORTER #2 (V.O.)

...Again, for everyone just tuning in, Theodore Steinberg, co-founder of the Magnus Pharmaceutical Corporation, has been shot during a live news conference and is in critical condition. The unknown assailant has also been killed. We've learned Steinberg is being treated in Magnus' own facilities. The Magnus Corporation is the creator of the new wonder-drug Eden, which has proven to reverse aging on the cellular level. In related news...

GRACE

He's still alive! Hugh, we need to go see Ted!

HUGH

We can't! They said he's in critical condition!

GRACE

He co-created the formula with your uncle! He could know something.

JOHNNY

If he's here, my guess is he's being held in the quarantine unit in the basement. It's like Magnus' own state of the art hospital.

HUGH

The basement? You think those creatures have gotten inside?

JOHNNY

We'll grab some weapons on the way down.

                    GRACE
The security room. That's where all the guards keep
their gear, right?

                    JOHNNY
Yeah, but we don't know if they already took all the
guns!

                    GRACE
Only one way to find out.

Hugh really doesn't like where this is going.

INT. HALLWAY OUTSIDE SECURITY ROOM - MOMENTS LATER
The three are headed to the security room, keeping a look out. Johnny breaks out
his cell phone, calls his aunt.

                    JOHNNY
Aunt Katherine, are you alright?

INTERCUT WITH -

INT. KATHERINE'S PANIC ROOM – SAME

                KATHERINE WALSH
Johnny! I'm fine. I got separated after the shooting and
security brought me to the chopper. What about you?

                JOHNNY (O.S.)
I'm okay. I'm with Hugh and Grace, we're headed down
to see Ted. Where are you?

KATHERINE WALSH

I'm in the panic room at home. Those creatures are all over the city. You three should come on over here. You'll be safe.

JOHNNY

We'll be there as soon as we can. Do you have a gun?

KATHERINE WALSH (V.O.)

Don't worry about me. Just get over he——-

JOHNNY

Aunt Katherine?

Johnny stares at his phone – Dead. He pockets it.

JOHNNY (CONT'D)

Battery's dead.

INT. SECURITY ROOM – magnus bldg - MOMENTS LATER
Most of the supplies in the room have already been ransacked. Some security camera screens are broken, casting the room in a flickering glow.

HUGH

Great. Now what?

GRACE

Come on, there are some lockers down this way.

Hugh stands off to a side as Johnny opens a few lockers, shaking his head, then he opens a fully-stocked one.

JOHNNY

Hello, what have we got here?

He draws out a pair of handguns and some ammo clips.

GRACE

Perfect. This should be alright.

JOHNNY

Oh, it gets better!

He pulls out an automatic shotgun, grinning deviously.

JOHNNY

Heeeeere's Johnny!

INT. MAGNUS ATRIUM - MOMENTS LATER

They arrive in the atrium, and not a moment too soon. Several zombies are outside in the parking lot, crawling over the cars.

A small hoard pound on the glass doors to the lobby, which begin to splinter and crack. Several corpses litter the area, torn apart. Grace looks at Hugh.

GRACE

Hugh...?

Hugh readies a gun. One of the zombies smashes through the glass door and makes a beeline for the three. Hugh holds the gun nervously, trying to get a clear shot.

BOOM! Hugh takes its head clean off with the shot. Hugh stands there, shocked by the kickback and the fact he just killed someone (even if it is a zombie).

HUGH

Whoa.

Johnny pats him on the back.

> JOHNNY
> Woo! Dude, you just popped your zombie cherry like
> a bad ass.
> (readies shotgun)
> Come on, you ugly undead fucks!

Two zombies approach him, and he fires his shotgun. The kickback literally knocks him off his feet.

His shot goes wild, and the zombie keeps storming towards him. Grace comes up behind the zombies and POP! POP! Blows their brains out. She helps Johnny to his feet and takes the shotgun from him, giving him the pistol.

> JOHNNY (CONT'D)
> Hey!

A wounded zombie on the floor groans and bites at the air. Grace plugs the zombie's mouth with the shotgun muzzle, the zombie's eyes bulge out with a scream, as she blasts its head to pieces.

Blood splatters all over her. She wipes her face.

> GRACE
> Rejuvenate that, you zombie fuck.

Hugh looks shocked from the attack.

INT. ELEVATOR - MOMENTS LATER
The three of them stand silent, stunned, armed, in the elevator, still splattered with blood. Light MUZAK and the DING of each floor the only sound, until –

> JOHNNY
> That. Was. Awesome! Better than a 3D video game!

GRACE

You couldn't even fire the damn rifle!

JOHNNY

At least I tried!

HUGH

We'll be sure to put that on your tombstone. Here lies
Johnny. He tried.

JOHNNY

Says the man whose girlfriend just-

DING!
The elevator doors open to the basement hospital – and it's crawling with zombies!

INT. BASEMENT HOSPITAL – MAGNUS HQ - CONTINUOUS
They all cock their guns and slowly step out of the elevator. But the zombies
are occupied – tearing apart the hospital rooms and closets searching for Eden!
They tear shit off the shelves like Black Friday at Walmart.

One finds a box of unused Eden syringes and they all tear the box apart,
injecting and eating what they can.

ZOMBIE #1

More! More!!!

Hugh, Grace and Johnny use the distraction to make their way to the end of the
corridor, making sure not to make a sound.

EXT. TED'S HOSPITAL ROOM - MOMENTS LATER
They find Ted in the last hospital room, his two security guards and a DOCTOR
dead and torn apart outside the door. Hugh grabs the keys from Security and
kicks their bodies out of the way.

INT. TED'S HOSPITAL ROOM – CONTINUOUS

They enter to find Ted hooked up to life support systems, his health is fading fast. A heart monitor beeps slowly. Grace is almost ready to cry and she runs to Ted's bedside.

> GRACE
> (choked up)

Oh, Ted!

> TED STEINBERG
> (opens his eyes)

Dr. Pilaro...

> (looks around)

Dr. Stephern... you're all right.

> JOHNNY

Uh, I'm here too.

> TED STEINBERG

Myers.

> (smiles slightly)

All of you, this whole disaster is my fault.

> GRACE

What are you talking about?

> TED STEINBERG

Eden. All of this trouble - it is all because of Eden.

> HUGH

That's impossible, we tested it and it worked!

TED STEINBERG

Years ago, Dr. Golden and I created the first Eden. We thought it worked too. But it turned a man into an abomination. People died.

GRACE

You knew this would happen?!

TED STEINBERG

I wanted to believe so badly that you had fixed it. That our life's work could live again and help the world. But I was kidding myself.

JOHNNY

Those things are looking for more Eden. They're like crack addicts.

GRACE

What?

HUGH

Addicts... no wonder it's selling so well. They're hooked on it. When we sold out, they—

GRACE

Started going through withdrawal. You think this is what happens on Eden withdrawal?

TED STEINBERG

This whole project was a mistake. That's why I tried to stop it. I couldn't let it happen again.

HUGH

Sir, it's all my fault! If I had only listened to you.

TED STEINBERG

It was never your fault, Hugh. I saw the tests. The formula worked perfectly. You did what your uncle couldn't. You would've made him proud.

HUGH

Then how did this happen?

TED STEINBERG
(coughing)
I don't know. We took every precaution.

HUGH

What should we do?

TED STEINBERG
(coughing worse)
Go back to the source. Everything you knew about Eden came from your uncle. Check his old records. Maybe they hold a cure. He had this whole secret lab he used to use.

Ted's monitor starts to go off.

GRACE

His blood pressure is spiking. His vitals are tanking.

HUGH

Ted? Where?

TED STEINBERG
(straining to speak)
...House.

His heart seizes and Ted trembles and goes silent. Dead. Grace closes his eyes and sheds a tear. Hugh and Johnny stand by, solemn.

                    HUGH
          We have to get back to my house.

                    JOHNNY
          Easier said than done.

Johnny looks out the locked door window when WHAM!!
    A mutilated Zombie face slaps against the other side, scaring the shit out of Johnny.

                    JOHNNY
          Any bright ideas, Doc?

Hugh looks at the zombies, the weapons, then back at Ted on his hospital bed. Grace notices.

                    GRACE
          No! No way. It's not right.

Hugh walks to Ted's bed, leans down to whisper in his ear.

                    HUGH
                  (whispers)
          You dedicated your life to saving people. Now you get
          to go out a hero one more time. And I'll make sure
          everyone knows it. I promise.

INT. BASEMENT HOSPITAL CORRIDOR – MAGNUS - MOMENTS LATER
The doors to Ted's hospital room smash open and Hugh and Grace, armed to the teeth, immediately start firing away, blasting Zombie brains to shit.

As a larger group of flesh-eaters races at them, Johnny comes from behind pushing Ted on his hospital bed at full speed.

Like a fucked up game of bowling, the bed knocks through a bunch of zombies, with a couple holding on for the ride.

Grace and Hugh keep shooting, killing many, as they race towards the elevator.

Once they get to the elevator and hit the button, there's still a half dozen zombies coming at them.

Hugh fires – CLICK! Empty.

DING! Elevator doors open just in time as Zombies grab at our three heroes. As they are cornered into the elevator, Johnny pushes Ted's hospital bed into the zombies one more time.

The left over zombies climb atop the bed to get to Hugh and Grace in the elevator and rip apart Ted's dead body, eating what they can.

GRACE

No!!!

Johnny pushes the bed further away. Grace screams as bloody pieces of Ted are hurled at the elevator doors as they finally close.

INT. ELEVATOR – CONTINUOUS

The three are once again silent, armed and bloody as the MUZAK can still be heard and the elevator DINGS as it arrives at the Lobby.

They exit to a momentarily quiet lobby. Together, they make their way towards the front doors. The RECEPTIONIST has been torn apart in her chair.

GRACE

Where are they?

JOHNNY

Any chance they realized there's no more Eden and went home?

DING!

The elevator behind them slowly opens and out pours a shit ton of hungry zombies. They chase our guys through the lobby towards the front door.

One Zombie jumps at Johnny, who grabs its head and bashes it into the large metal sculpture in the middle of the lobby, shattering its face.

JOHNNY

So gross.

They race outside towards the parking lot, slamming the door behind them. They put a random BLOODY ARM they find through the handle so the zombies can't open it, locking them inside.

EXT. MAGNUS HQ – AFTERNOON - CONTINUOUS

Outside, Hugh & Co. see a number of soldiers, cops and regular citizens battling with zombies.

Nearby, three soldiers are being overwhelmed by zombies. One of the soldiers has a small tablet computer, sending messages to a command center.

SOLDIER #1

There are too many! We need to fall back!

SOLDIER WITH TABLET

We've lost the comms! Keep firing!

They try to defend their position but the marauding zombies plow through them, ripping them apart. The soldier with the tablet is left a broken, bloody mess. He grabs the tablet and with bloodied fingers taps a final message to command: "OVRRRUN. ZOMBYTES ON MOV." Then dies.

The zombie reaches for the tablet, sees its hideous reflection in the screen, touches its face, SCREAMS out and SMASHES the tablet screen.

The zombie turns to Hugh, Grace and Johnny, who watched the carnage. When they see the zombie notice them, they book it towards the cars.

                          HUGH
Go! Move! Move!

                 COL. KILPATRICK (PRE-LAP)
Move it! Let's go!

INT. ABANDONED ARMANTI RECORDS BUILDING - AFTERNOON
The National Guard has taken over the old, iconic Armanti Records building. At the top of the building, COLONEL GORDON A. KILPATRICK,
a bull and beast of a commander, is overseeing the setup of a command
station.

                     COL. KILPATRICK
I want those comm systems set up now! This isn't a
goddamn field exercise, people! This is war!

The soldiers double-time getting equipment in. He picks up a ringing phone.

                 COL. KILPATRICK (CONT'D)
Kilpatrick here.

                 COMMANDER RIGGS (O.S.)
Sir, we're getting reports of civilian uprisings in the
Westwood and Ladera areas. They're looting and burn-
ing stores.

                     COL. KILPATRICK
Commander, anyone who's out there hindering instead
of helping, I want them shot on sight.

                 COMMANDER RIGGS (V.O.)
Sir? You can't be serious!

COL. KILPATRICK

You're damn right I'm serious! This ain't a job for civil-
ians, soldier. You got that?!

He hangs up the phone and gets onto a comms console. It comes alive with information. Several red spots are showing up on a map of Los Angeles. Several
soldiers are also manning some consoles in the room.

COL. KILPATRICK (CONT'D)

Lieutenant!

A soldier comes over. He's younger than Kilpatrick.

LT. HAMMOND

Sir! Reports coming in from Beverly Hills and
Westwood, the Zombytes have overrun our defenses.

COL. KILPATRICK

The what now?

LT. HAMMOND

That's what they're calling them now, sir. Zombytes.

COL. KILPATRICK

I don't care what they're calling them, just kill them! I
need boots on the ground in these areas.
(pointing to map)
Set up five miles from the edge of each perimeter of the
infected zones from the north and south and start pushing in. We'll squeeze out those diseased pukes from every
hot spot. Use whatever we got. And get me another team
to take to Magnus HQ on the double. If that's where these
fuckers are coming from, we'll fry 'em at the source.

LT. HAMMOND

Sir, we don't have enough men to cover those areas.

COL. KILPATRICK

(slams the table)

Just do it! Restore order at all costs.

The Lieutenant hesitates, while the colonel gets impatient.

COL. KILPATRICK (CONT'D)

...What are you waiting for, an invitation?! Move!

The lieutenant leaves. Kilpatrick stares at the screen.

COL. KILPATRICK (CONT'D)

We're coming, you blood-thirsty bastards.

EXT. MAGNUS PARKING LOT – SAME

The trio makes a run for it, only shooting the zombies that get in the way and Grace smashes one in the face with the butt of her rifle.

They run for the SUV and Johnny finally opens it with a CHIRP CHIRP.

INT. JOHNNY'S SUV - CONTINUOUS

Everyone piles up into the car. Several zombies begin to swarm around them.

Zombie hands bang at the window to grab them. Hugh starts the SUV, as the zombies start to rock it back and forth. Hugh is terrified.

JOHNNY

What are you waiting for? Come on!

A zombie breaks through the front passenger window, grabbing at Grace. She SCREAMS, and the zombie pulls her out of the window halfway. She still has the shotgun, and BLASTS the zombie at point blank range, getting back into the SUV.

But others have taken its cue and now SMASH through the windows and grab and bite at the three sitting ducks.

                    GRACE
        Go! Go! Go!

Suddenly, THWACK THWACK THWACK PSHOO PSHOO –

The Zombytes are taken apart. Johnny looks through the back window – it's a TEAM of SOLDIERS on jeeps with roof-mounted mini-guns coming over the hill towards Magnus.

In one of those Jeeps manning the big gun sits Col. Kilpatrick. He's a kid in a candy store – if the kid got to shoot the candy with a big gun.

Unfortunately, as they SHOOT, bullets hit the SUV everywhere - including the gas tank, which starts leaking.

Another slew of shots and the final parking lot Zombies SCREAM as a fire ignites near the undercarriage of the SUV.

                    JOHNNY
        Ah shit! Get out! Get out! It's gonna blow!

Hugh, Grace and Johnny jump out of the car as the bullets stop and they run for cover as – BOOOOOM!

The car explodes in a bright fireball.

The military jeeps and Kilpatrick just keep going towards the building, not giving them a second thought.

                    HUGH
        Shit! There goes our ride.

                    JOHNNY
        Ah, man! You think insurance covers zombie attacks?

> GRACE
>
> If the military is gonna take our ride, maybe we should
> take one of theirs.

Grace points to a military Mp5 truck sitting in the parking lot. The only thing near it is a zombie with no legs, munching on the body of a dead soldier. They run towards it and Hugh shoots the zombie in the head at point-blank range -- even he couldn't miss it.

Hugh steps over the zombie's body and into the truck, looking around. The engine is still running and the keys are still in the ignition.

Grace hops into the front passenger seat and Johnny gets in the back. Hugh looks around at the dash and the gearshift nervously. He doesn't drive stick.

> GRACE
>
> Hugh, come on!

Hugh hits the gas, but nothing happens. He fumbles around the gearshift, trying to make it move. Finally, the truck jolts in reverse, running over a Zombyte. Hugh shifts the gear again, and the truck goes zooming out of the lot.

INT. MP5 MILITARY TRUCK - CONTINUOUS
Hugh drives erratically on city surface streets while avoiding civilian looters and gang bangers having a shootout with Zombytes. Hugh swerves to avoid some gunfire and heads into the downtown area of Los Angeles.

> HUGH
>
> You guys alright?!

> GRACE
>
> Peachy. Damn recoil bruised my arm.

HUGH

Johnny, you okay back there?

REAR OF TRUCK -

Johnny sits up and looks at Hugh and Grace through the open window directly behind the driver and passenger seat.

JOHNNY

Yeah I'm good. That was close, man.

Johnny looks down to his feet to see open crates of ammunition, a few sets of M16 machine gun rifles, some road flares, a box of grenade rounds with a grenade launcher, a barrel of black crude oil, some C4 explosives and a small RPG launcher.

JOHNNY (CONT'D)

Fuck me!

HUGH

What?!

JOHNNY

We're stocked with explosives back here!

HUGH

What?!

JOHNNY

The good news is, we got weapons! Bad news - we're driving a bomb!

HUGH

Great... just gets better!

Suddenly they hear on the CB Scanner a report coming in from the command center. Hugh turns on the truck's radio.

> LT. HAMMOND (V.O.)
> Attention citizens of Los Angeles County. This is Lt. Hammond speaking. The creatures called Zombytes are still being suppressed by the National Guard. All citizens are advised to stay indoors at all times and comply with federal officers regarding your safety. If you see the creatures please make no attempt to fight them. This broadcast will be repeated every fifteen minutes, and shelters will be listed shortly.

Hugh turns down the volume after the report ends.

EXT. WILSHIRE BLVD. - AFTERNOON

Hugh drives the truck down a rubble-laden street while a National Guard contingent is battling some Zombytes from an abandoned storefront. The Zombytes tear through them mercilessly.

An Army jeep careens down the street behind Hugh's truck, with two Zombytes hanging on the sides. One Zombyte bites into the driver's neck, spilling blood everywhere. The soldier driving SCREAMS.

The jeep swerves and the other soldier, a FEMALE, shoots the Zombyte off the jeep and quickly takes the wheel. As she drives, however, she begins to go into spasms.

She reaches into a pocket and pulls out a spent Eden syringe.

> FEMALE SOLDIER
> Oh Christ, not now!

The driver starts to go into more spasms and the jeep swerves more as she TURNS.

INT. MP5 MILITARY TRUCK - AFTERNOON

Hugh looks in the mirror at the Army jeep right behind them. He can see the female Zombyte in combat uniform driving the jeep, and it's speeding up.

The jeep slams into the back of the truck, sending Hugh and Grace jumping in their seats. In the back Johnny is bounced around on the crates. He yells.

EXT. WILSHIRE BLVD/MP5 TRUCK - SAME

The Zombyte driving the jeep slams into the truck again, growling in rage.

> JOHNNY
> Hugh, we got a zombie on our ass!

> HUGH
> Well, do something about it!

> JOHNNY
> Like what?

> HUGH
> I don't know... throw something at it for fuck's sake!

Johnny looks around for a weapon, and opens a crate of grenades. He fumbles with the pin, pulls it out and quickly throws the grenade at the jeep.

The jeep explodes in a massive fireball, and the truck gets away. Johnny takes cover as Hugh heaves a sigh.

EXT. HOLLYWOOD – MINUTES LATER

Zombies roam the streets in packs, and Hugh drives right through or around them. Occasionally, they pass a police or National Guard roadblock.

They drive past some police in riot gear shooting tear gas into a group of zombies, but the zombies get even more aggressive. One zombie throws the gas canister back, and the rest charge at the cops as they open fire.

Hugh stops the truck about a block away from the battle.

HUGH

Johnny!

JOHNNY

Already on it, Doc. FIRE IN THE HOLE!!

Johnny grabs the Grenade launcher. He grabs a grenade, pulls the pin and LAUNCHES it at the voracious zombie clan.

BOOM! Carnage everywhere, but they've saved the police and military under attack.

Hugh drives on, a salute to the military as they pass.

EXT. MACARTHUR PARK – minutes later

The sun sets in an orange, smoke-filled sky. The truck is starts to slow down and sputter. It's a bad part of town.

Several Zombytes are poke their heads out from around rubble or windows.

INT. MP5 MILITARY TRUCK - AFTERNOON

Hugh looks at the dashboard. The fuel gauge reads empty.

GRACE

What's going on?

HUGH

We're out of gas.

GRACE

Shit. Maybe we could take the subway? Is there a train station near your place?

HUGH

I don't know, who takes the train in LA? Wait, yeah, I think there is one actually.

She points to a nearby subway entrance. Hugh pulls the truck over as it coughs and dies.

                    JOHNNY
          Are the trains still running?

                    HUGH
          We'll know soon enough. Johnny, what other weapons
          are back there?

Johnny rummages around the crates.

                    JOHNNY
          Some charges for the C4, some ammo clips, some big
          rifles, and... Whoa! Holy shit!

                    HUGH

                    What?

EXT. MP5 MILITARY TRUCK/SUBWAY ENTRANCE - CONTINUOUS
Johnny steps out of the truck's back with a flamethrower strapped to his back.
He's grinning like a madman.

                    JOHNNY
          Johnny 5 Alive!

Hugh grumbles, and grabs some C4 and a rifle. Thankfully, it's already loaded.
He pulls back the slide.

                    GRACE
          Do you even know how to use that?

HUGH

Shouldn't be that much different --Grace, get down!

Grace ducks. In an instant, he scores a perfect headshot on a Zombyte from thirty feet away. Grace gets up and looks with bewilderment.

JOHNNY

Headshot!

Hugh stifles a smile. Maybe he is becoming a leader after all. However, six more Zombytes appear among the ruins and charge right at them!

They start to backtrack towards the subway entrance as Johnny lets loose with his flamethrower. The Zombytes are ignited instantly and they flail about as the flames consume their mutated bodies.

Hugh dares to get close to one Zombyte that is partially burned. It lies on its back, twitching. It looks right at Hugh with bulging, bloodshot eyes.

ZOMBYTE

Help us... please !

Hugh can't believe it. A Zombyte just talked to him! Grace comes to his side as Hugh readies his pistol at the Zombyte's head.

HUGH

I'm sorry.

Hugh shoots the Zombyte point-blank.

INT. SUBWAY STAIRWAY - EVENING

The three head down the stairs into the dim-lit subway tunnel. The power is out and the train has stopped running. The three move through the subway corridor cautiously.

GRACE

There should be a fuse box somewhere around here.

Suddenly, three large and deformed Zombytes pop out of the shadows and attack them! Hugh yells.

Hugh unleashes a barrage of machine gun fire, downing two Zombytes. The last Zombyte lunges at Grace knocking her down. She is too terrified to move, frozen with fear.

BANG! The large Zombyte falls to the ground dead as Hugh lowers his smoking rifle. It's a clean shot to the head. Grace smiles slightly and Hugh helps her up.

GRACE (CONT'D)

Thanks.

HUGH

Anytime.

JOHNNY

Here we go, love birds.

Johnny finds the fuse box in the entry tunnel and hits the emergency restore. Power returns to the station and the subway can run again. The doors open for them, and they hop aboard.

The train takes off speeding through the dark tunnel to the next station near Wilshire and Western.

INT. TRAIN CAR - EVENING

The three rest inside the car and sit, taking a breather. Johnny takes off the heavy flamethrower tank from his back.

HUGH

That thing. Outside. It said "Help us." It SAID "Help Us."

GRACE

We're doing all we can, Hugh.

Hugh holds his head down in shame. His body is quivering.

HUGH

This is all my fault!

GRACE

No it isn't, Hugh. You heard what Ted told you.

HUGH

I made everyone like this! I turned all those people into addicts just like me! Once a junkie, always a junkie.

Grace shakes Hugh out of it.

GRACE

Hugh! Listen to me! It wasn't your fault. Ted said everything was squared away before production!

HUGH

What if he was wrong?

GRACE

Don't talk like that! We're going to fix this, but you need to focus.

Hugh takes a deep breath, looks into Grace's eyes and nods.

INT. SUBWAY STATION/STAIRWAY - MOMENTS LATER
The train comes to a stop at Wilshire and Western. The trio exits the train, watching out for zombies, and runs up the steps to the street.

JOHNNY

Gotta love a train system that cost billions to build and
only has 4 stops.

EXT. SUBWAY STATION – EVENING - CONTINUOUS

The three, armed to the teeth, take bad Charlie's Angels poses as they exit the
station and look around for zombies – but it's clear.

Explosions and screams can be heard off in the distance, but the streets
around them seem to be clear.

HUGH

Okay, my Uncle's – I mean, my place – is just a few
blocks away. Stay alert, stay together. Let's go.

INT. MAGNUS HQ – HOSPITAL BASEMENT - SAME

Kilpatrick and Walter walk side by side down the glass windowed halls. In various rooms, a few scientists in EDS suits work on living Zombyte specimens.

A few Zombytes are chained to gurneys, screaming. The glass wall in front
of them blocks out some of the noise.

COL. KILPATRICK

Disgusting sons of bitches. How does something like
this happen?

WALTER STEINBERG

The sick are the greatest danger for the healthy.

They watch a Zombyte being dissected. The Zombyte shrieks so loud that the
scientists cover their ears.

COL. KILPATRICK

I'm losing men every hour thanks to those freaks! You
better have brought me down here for more than show
and tell.

WALTER STEINBERG

I brought you down here to show you there's a bigger plan in place. You need to trust me.

COL. KILPATRICK

No, I don't. If we can't take full control of the situation soon, DC is gonna send nukes flying, and the whole country goes to hell! Infected or not, Los Angeles will burn. And it won't end there.

WALTER STEINBERG

Is that really such a bad thing?

Kilpatrick stops short at this, shocked. Walter looks back.

COL. KILPATRICK

You're not paying me enough to watch the world get torn apart.

WALTER STEINBERG

Oh no? How much does that cost? Cause last I checked, you and your men haven't had any problems cashing the checks. But if Eden dries out, so does your big military contract.

Kilpatrick pulls a gun on Walter, aiming it at his forehead. Walter isn't scared. Secured Zombytes in the background are still going crazy.

COL. KILPATRICK

You think this is all about money?! Damn you, Steinberg! People are getting ripped apart by those things! My people!

WALTER STEINBERG

If anyone understands the cost of war, Colonel, it's you. That's why I called you. Think of it this way – what kind of people bought Eden in the first place? The useless elderly looking to squeeze a few more desperate years in and the utterly vain and superficial trying to defy God and time itself.

A more perfect union. It's what we both want. For that to happen, we need to keep the Eden coming. Your men can contain and kill the Zombytes as they see fit. But they will not interfere with the bigger picture. Is that understood?

Kilpatrick hesitates, then holsters his weapon.

COL. KILPATRICK

And what would happen to your precious Magnus if the press found out what you're doing?

WALTER STEINBERG (CONT'D)

You know what would happen? We'd be vilified, condemned and discredited. Then we'd come up with a new miracle cure for blue balls or saggy tits and the world would love us all over again... Now imagine what would happen if the world found out that the U.S. Military is nothing more than the chained-up dog of a pharmaceutical company. Guns for hire to the highest bidder. Which do you think would be the bigger story?

Kilpatrick lets that resonate for a moment, then -

COL. KILPATRICK

Every war needs an enemy we can kill, and another one
we can blame. You're the new CEO of Magnus so right
now that makes you IT.

Walter realizes he's right. As the two walk towards a quieter empty hospital
room, Walter pulls out his cell phone and dials.

INTERCUT AS NECESSARY WITH –

EXT. LOS ANGELES STREETS – EVENING – SAME
Hugh, Grace and Johnny are making their way through the all-too-quiet streets
on their way to Hugh's.

   Hugh hears the loud RINGTONE, which scares the crap out of him and he
fumbles for the phone and picks up.

HUGH (V.O.)

Hello?

WALTER STEINBERG

Hugh! It's Walt. Haven't heard from you since the shit
hit. How you doin'?

HUGH

Little busy, Walter. Ya know, what with the zombie in-
vasion and end of the world and all.

WALTER STEINBERG
Yeah, total bummer. Where are you right now?

HUGH

On our way to try and find a way to fix this... Look, Walter, I'm sorry about your dad. But he said there might be something wrong with the formula, so we--

WALTER STEINBERG

Have you mentioned this to anyone else?

HUGH (V.O.)

No. It's just me, Grace, and Johnny.

WALTER STEINBERG

Listen to me, Hugh. We're working on it right now. We'll get this sorted out, okay? Why don't you just go somewhere and lay low, alright?

HUGH

No offense, Walter, but this is out of your hands now. We need to figure out what caused this if we have any hope to reverse it.

WALTER STEINBERG

Hugh, just tell me where you are and we can—

HUGH

Sorry, I gotta go, Walt. Stay safe.

Walter hangs up, thinks a beat, and turns to Kilpatrick.

WALTER STEINBERG

Colonel, maybe it's time I tell you about the people who thought up the formula and are responsible for its production.

              COL. KILPATRICK

I'm listening.

              WALTER STEINBERG

Doctors Hugh Stephern and Grace Pilaro. You want your poster boys for this outbreak? You want your cure? Find them and bring them here. Preferably alive.

EXT. HUGH'S HOUSE - EVENING

Hugh and crew arrive outside Hugh's home, which thankfully has been left untouched by Zombytes or looters.

              JOHNNY

This is where you live?

              HUGH

Yeah. Sorry it's not like Katherine's, but it's all I got.

A loud mess of SCREAMS suddenly ring out from the West. They're coming.

              GRACE

Let's get the hell off the streets.

INT. HUGH'S HOUSE - EVENING

The three enter and Grace and Johnny look around at Hugh's Uncle's house. It's still cluttered with books and boxes.

              HUGH

Well, at least the power's still on.

From O.S. they hear a guttural growl coming from the bedroom. Angry.

JOHNNY

Jesus, they're inside!

HUGH

No! Wait. It's just Herbie. He's probably starving.

JOHNNY

Yeah, for flesh. Wasn't he the first test subject? He could be all Zombie-dog now.

HUGH

Only one way to find out.

They approach the closed bedroom door as the growling continues on the other side. Johnny cocks his gun.

Standing to the side of the door, Johnny nods as Hugh grabs the knob and slowly turns and PUSHES the door wide open.

WOOF! Out jumps Herbie – totally fine and licking Hugh's face. They all take a deep breath of relief.

HUGH

Aw, I bet you're hungry, huh boy? Come on, let's get you some treats.

LIVING ROOM – MOMENTS LATER

Johnny looks at Hugh's collection of anime paraphernalia, laughing. Johnny collapses on a sofa. Herbert nuzzles him.

JOHNNY

Ahh a couch has never felt so good.

Johnny turns on the holographic TV. It's another news report, but the audio is cut, replaced with an alarm sound. It's the Emergency Broadcast System, and it says

"LOS ANGELES AREA UNDER QUARANTINE, ALL FREEWAYS ARE SHUT DOWN UNTIL FURTHER NOTICE."
Hugh and Grace begin to go through the boxes of journals and papers that Hugh had looked through earlier.

> JOHNNY
>
> You guys keep looking, I'm gonna make some food.

TIME CUT –

INT. UNCLE'S STUDY/HUGH'S LAB
All three snack on food as they go through everything they can find, to no avail.

> HUGH
>
> It's pointless. There's nothing. Ted said my Uncle had
> his own home lab, but there's nothing here.

> GRACE
>
> Maybe we're just not looking in the
> right place.

Grace puts down a stack of papers and begins to search the walls for trap doors, KNOCKING for the hollow sound.
   She walks out of the room. Hugh and Johnny look at each other and then follow after her.

HALLWAY –
They all knock on walls all over the house.

BATHROOM –
Johnny knocks around.

KITCHEN –
Grace knocks around.

BEDROOM CLOSET –
Hugh KNOCKS and – it has a hollow back. He feels around and pulls off a false panel to reveal a door to –

HENRY GOLDEN'S PRIVATE LAB

HUGH
Guys! I found something!

INT. HG GOLDEN'S SECRET LAB – MOMENTS LATER
The equipment in the lab is covered with dust and wear, years of neglect. Dell Desktops. It's very 1990.

There's an old safe in the corner. Hugh finds a crowbar and breaks it open. Inside is another journal and stacks of papers and photos detailing the Eden Formula as well as before and after photos of RODNEY, the first subject.

HUGH
I think we found something.

GRACE
Let me take a look at that.

Grace reads the journal, inspecting it carefully.

GRACE (CONT'D)
This journal came from Ted Steinberg. Looks like after
one of their subject tests went awry, they abandoned the
project completely. But...hmm, a binary compound...
(reads)
"We realize maintaining the formula's integri-
ty requires recognition of those elements which,
through experimentation, yielded negative results or

unanticipated withdrawals. Therefore, to maximize Eden's results, we charted those ingredients and methods which nullified or mutated the formula's effects."

JOHNNY

In English?

GRACE

During the formula's original creation, there was a system set up so they could keep track of which things would counter the effects of Eden; to reverse the process.

HUGH

So in theory, we could figure out which element caused the mutation and could make an antidote out of that. Or at least find a way to remove it from the formula.

JOHNNY

What, because some ancient book in a safe told you? And even if it did work, and it can cure these things, how could you get it to <u>all</u> of them? What do we do, go up to every zombie and shoot them up with it?

HUGH

We'll have to cross that bridge when we come to it. For now, we have a bigger bridge to cross.

Grace already knows where he's going. Johnny's lost.

HUGH

We're gonna need a sample.

JOHNNY

I'll chug a beer and be ready in a few.

HUGH

Not that kind of sample. Someone needs to go out there and get a sample of their blood and skin.

Grace and Hugh both look at Johnny.

JOHNNY

Fuck that, it's a war zone out there!

HUGH

Without studying a blood and skin sample, we can't know which strain of Eden they are infected with. Or how to cure it.

JOHNNY

I'm not your assistant anymore.

HUGH

You're right. You're our partner.

Johnny looks from Johnny to Grace, who nods.

JOHNNY

Alright, let's do this. But I'm not going out there unprotected.

EXT. HUGH'S HOUSE – MINUTES LATER

There are now a few roving Zombytes in the street. They seem to be search-ing for something, as they smash car windows and attack anything in their way.

Johnny opens the front door and steps onto the porch wearing an old football helmet, a couple holstered guns, and the flame thrower. He shuts the door behind him.

> JOHNNY
> One undead test subject extra crispy, coming up.

He slowly walks towards the street.

INT. HUGH'S HOUSE - SAME
Meanwhile in the lab, Hugh and Grace get to work. Hugh boots up his computers and starts looking through the files at Magnus. They ready the labs, mix chemicals and use the old equipment.
  Herbie comes in, still spry and happy. He nudges Hugh's arm.

> HUGH
> Go play, boy. Daddy's busy.

He throws a ball and Herbie runs after it.

> HUGH
> Still can't believe Herbie's so... Wait a sec. Herbie's still young and he didn't turn. No adverse withdrawal symptoms. My original formula *did* work. It's still working. That means—

BANG! BANG! BANG! Grace and Hugh run to the front door, grabbing their guns just in case. They open to find -
  Johnny stands there holding a dismembered and bloody Zombyte arm like a dog who found a bone. He hands it to Hugh.

> JOHNNY
> Special delivery! One bloody zombie stump as requested. Boom! No need to thank--

Suddenly A ZOMBYTE jumps on Johnny from behind, biting into his shoulder. Johnny SCREAMS!

Johnny turns, grabs his gun and all three fire bullets into the monster, who tumbles down the porch, dead.

They slam and lock the door, but Johnny's bleeding like a bitch.

GRACE

Shit. I'll get bandages and tape.

JOHNNY

Mother fucker! Where the hell did he come from?

Johnny heads to the couch, keeping pressure on his wound.

HUGH

Um, that's a new couch.

Johnny glares at him, incredulous.

HUGH (CONT'D)

Right. No worries.

Grace returns with gauze, bandages and tape. She cleans the area, applies pressure and bandages him up.

GRACE

You sure you're okay?

JOHNNY

Takes more than a nibble to keep me down. Go, do your science thing. I may need that antidote sooner than later.

INT. ABANDONED LAB - MOMENTS LATER
Hugh takes a syringe and gets the blood sample from the arm.

Using a centrifuge, which spins rapidly to separate chemicals, Hugh extracts a clear liquid from the blood and looks at it under a microscope.

MICROSCOPE POV
The microscope shows traces of a chemical compound floating in a clear liquid.

BACK TO SCENE
Hugh rifles through the journal, then turns to Grace.

> HUGH
> Grace, when we had Eden ready, did we cap it off with the enzyme inhibitor?

> GRACE
> Um... yeah, I'm pretty sure we did.

> HUGH
> Yeah, you see... the Eden that I just found from the blood sample? It doesn't have that.

> GRACE
> It doesn't?

> HUGH
> Not at all. I recognize its structure, but this isn't the one that we certified after the human trials. Or the one I gave Herbie.

> GRACE
> Do you think the formula got degraded somehow with all the production?

HUGH

That, or it wasn't the right formula to begin with.

Hugh looks up different sequences, algorithms and holographic visuals on the computer, comparing them to his Uncle's old journals and computer files and Magnus's.

HUGH

I got it!

GRACE

What?

Hugh points at the 3-D computer image. There are two rotating chemical models, one different than the other. One is marked "V.1.2.045" and the other is marked "V.1.8.946".

HUGH
(points to one on the right)
This is the version of Eden that went through the test, the one that succeeded. MY formula.

GRACE

Okay...

HUGH
(points to one on the left)
And this is the one from the Zombyte. It's an earlier version, like I said, but it's also really unstable. Check out my Uncle's notes:
(reading from the screen)
"V.1.2.045 serum injection resulted in massive cellular deterioration unless given in massive regular

doses. Affected mental capacity of test subject, physical deformities settling in, subject became violent and uncontrollable."

JOHNNY

In other words, became a junkie.

This hits Hugh.

HUGH

Just like the monkey.

GRACE

It doesn't make sense. How did that version go into production?

HUGH

I don't know. Maybe some intern hit the wrong key and got them mixed up.

Hugh sits down and thinks harder.

HUGH (CONT'D)

Or maybe...someone did it on purpose. Someone could've switched the formulas after we signed off.

GRACE

Why?

HUGH

To sabotage us? Bring down the company? I don't know. But at least now we know how to make the antidote.

LATER -

Hugh and Grace are still working on creating the antidote, calibrating and checking blood samples and running tests.

In the next room, Johnny keeps watching TV and keeping pressure on his wound when images of Hugh and Grace come on the screen, and the words "WANTED FOR BIO-TERRORISM."

JOHNNY

Uh... guys?

HUGH

Not now, Johnny. We're almost done with the cure.

JOHNNY

You guys are on TV!

Hugh and Grace look over their shoulders to see the hologram playing and their WANTED faces. Johnny turns the volume up.

NEWS REPORTER (O.S.)

Though Dr. Stephern has yet to be brought to justice, we're outside his father's house. Let's see if he'll speak with us.

The Reporter knocks on the door. Hugh groans as his father, Morgan, opens up and is live on camera.

NEWS REPORTER (O.S.)

Evening, sir. What can you tell us about your son, now a wanted bio-terrorist? Are you shocked?

MORGAN STEPHERN

A terrorist? Give me a break! He's no terrorist.

Hugh is surprised – maybe he'll defend him after all.

MORGAN STEPHERN (CONT'D)
He's a fuck-up. I'd be *shocked* if he was able to pull off something like this. Believe me - if this is his fault, it wasn't on purpose. He has screwed up everything he's ever done. Guess this time, everyone is paying for his failure. Hugh, if you're watching this, turn yourself in. You're not smart enough to get away.

Morgan slams the door on the reporter. Grace groans.

JOHNNY
Well, that could've been worse.

Grace and Hugh look at him. He shrugs.

GRACE
We need to finish the antidote.

HUGH
It's mixing right now. Should be done in a few minutes. Only thing is, we still need to test it.

JOHNNY
Don't look at me. I'm done playing guinea pig for to-day, thank you.

Johnny walks away, back over to the couch.

GRACE
(to Hugh)
Let's say this deadly addictive formula was switched on purpose. Why would they release it like that?

                            HUGH
Because then people would be forced to buy it just so
they wouldn't turn into monsters. Don't you get it?

                            GRACE
But the public didn't KNOW it would do that. So who
would have?

                            HUGH
Who else? Katherine! She has the most to gain.

Grace turns to Johnny, but he's watching TV again and not listening.

                            GRACE
Now way. I don't buy it.

                            HUGH
She knew about the project since day one, and she
would've wanted people to get addicted to Eden to
keep the money flowing.

                            GRACE
We can't prove any of that.

                            HUGH
I know...
                            (sighs)
The proof will all be at Magnus. But it's right in the
middle of the city. How the hell do we get there?

EXT. HUGH'S HOUSE – NIGHT
The group looks around at the smashed-up cars on the curb.

                              HUGH
        We'll take one of those.

Hugh clears the glass out of one car's windows, unlocks it and gets in. He pulls
off the cover beneath the steering wheel to expose some wires where the ignition
switch is. Johnny looks at Grace.

                             JOHNNY
        Do I want to know how you know how to do that?

Hugh gets up from the car. The engine is running.

                              HUGH
        I used to live on the streets. Old habits die hard. Now
        let's get out of here.

Grace and Johnny pile into the car, and they take off.

INT. ARMANTI RECORDS BUILDING - NIGHT
Kilpatrick is on a call with Walter. The National Guardsmen watch holographic
readouts and night-vision screens of the ensuing battles around Los Angeles.

                    WALTER STEINBERG (V.O.)
        We need those two scientists, Colonel, and we need
        them now. How close are you to finding them?

                       COL. KILPATRICK
        Any minute, Steinberg, relax. Soldiers should be knock-
        ing down his door any second.

He hangs up, and turns to a large computer screen. A 3-D image shows up – a squad
of soldiers closing in on a building. Armed, night vision goggles on, they converge.

                        COL. KILPATRICK (CONT'D)
                              (smiling)
         Got you.

INT. HUGH'S HOUSE - MOMENTS LATER
The Soldiers burst into Hugh's home. They sweep around doing a perimeter
check.

                           GUARDSMAN #1
         Clear!

                           GUARDSMAN #2
                          (checking kitchen)
         Clear!

                           LT. HAMMOND
                          (checking the lab)
         Clear!

They keep looking. Only Herbert the dog is in the apartment and he's not
talking.

                           GUARDSMAN #1
         Sir, there's nobody in here!

The Lieutenant pounds the wall angrily, speaks into his Comm.

                           LT. HAMMOND
         Sorry Colonel, we lost them.

He walks around the living room and sees a paper posted on the TV with writ-
ing on it.

LT. HAMMOND (CONT'D)
Wait a second, sir. I think there's something here you
need to see.

INSERT – PAPER ON TV –

"WE ARE INNOCENT. FRAMED BY MAGNUS.
WE HAVE THE CURE."

INT. STOLEN CAR - SAME
Hugh, in the hotwired car, drives them back towards Magnus, passing several
National Guard roadblocks. Johnny's shoulder is starting to bleed through his
bandages.

Straight ahead there's a group of Zombytes. Hugh guns it.

GRACE PILARO
Oh my God, you're not going to...

HUGH STEPHERN
Hang on!

They hang on for dear life as Hugh plows right through the Zombytes in a
massive gooey explosion of blood and body parts. The car gets dented and the
windshield gets cracked.

As they recover, Grace looks up ahead.

GRACE PILARO
Look out!

UP AHEAD IN STREET –
There is a massive National Guard roadblock, with armored personnel carriers
and tanks. Soldiers are lined up to stop any oncoming traffic. But there is a hole.

                    SOLDIER (O.S.)
                   (into megaphone)
      Stop your car immediately! This is a restricted area!

IN CAR –

Hugh can't stop now. He digs in, speeding up.

                      SOLDIER
                   (into megaphone)
      I repeat. Stop your vehicle or we will shoot!

                       GRACE

      Um, Hugh?

                        HUGH

      Fuck it. Come too far now. Hold on.

The soldiers raise their weapons and begin FIRING!

    Grace and Johnny duck down as Hugh swerves between their roadblocks, dodging the soldiers and their shots. The car gets riddled with bullets but somehow makes it through.

INT. STOLEN CAR - CONTINUOUS

Johnny, wincing, looks in the rear windshield. The soldiers start their jeeps and begin to follow.

                      JOHNNY

      Uh, I think you made 'em mad.

Hugh makes some quick turns, trying to lose the soldiers. The car begins to smoke and sputter. Shot to shit. He sees an alleyway up ahead and on the other side of it - a LARGE UNMANNED TANK in the middle of the road.

Hugh turns the car, fish-tailing, and zooms it down the alley, knocking shit everywhere. It's a tight fit. The Soldier's Jeeps race right by the alley behind them.

The car stalls halfway down the alley – dead. Hugh and Company ditch the car and run towards the tank. Not seeing any soldiers around, Hugh crawls under the tank, and finds an access hatch in its underbelly.

HUGH

> Under here!

Grace and Johnny crawl under and climb up into the tank.

INT. TANK

The tank seems smaller on the inside than it does outside. The room is corrugated steel and very cramped conditions. Ammo boxes are lined inside the room, and there is an alcove off to a side where the pilot and copilot sit.

Someone is already in there -- a TANK DRIVER.

TANK DRIVER

> What the hell? Who are you?

Hugh bolts to the driver and puts a gun to his head.

HUGH

> Listen to me. We're not going to hurt you, but you need
> to take us to the Magnus building.

TANK DRIVER

> Does this look like fucking Uber to you? Not a chance!

The Tank Driver goes to pull a sidearm, but Hugh wrestles it away and keeps his gun pointed at his head.

                    HUGH
    I won't ask nicely again!

The Tank Driver sees he's serious. He grabs the controls of the tank. Johnny
hops in the copilot seat.

                    HUGH
        What are you doing?

                    JOHHNY
        You kidding? I'm not missing out on this. Who knows
        how much longer I got.

The tank lurches forward.

EXT. LOS ANGELES STREETS - MOMENTS LATER
The National Guardsmen see the tank moving down the street and are confused
at first.

                GUARDSMAN #3
        Hey, who's driving that thing?

                GUARDSMAN #4
    I dunno.
                (gets on comms)
        Whoever's in that tank, you are not authorized to go
        past the perimeter! Stop now!

The tank does not yield and keeps moving away from the blockade. The
Guardsmen chase it in an APC, shooting at the armored beast to no affect. Then
one GUARDSMAN takes out a grenade and pulls the pin.

INT. TANK -

The tank is rocked by the grenade explosion, but the Tank Driver and Johnny keep the vehicle moving. Grace, thrown about by the explosion, bounces off the steel walls. She yelps in fear.

Hugh catches Grace and holds her close.

> HUGH
> We're almost out of here, baby, don't worry!
> (turns to Johnny)
> You think you can work the cannon on this thing?

Johnny grins wide.

> JUMP CUT TO:

Johnny is in the cannon turret and rotates the cannon several degrees around, pointing at the APC. The cannon is automatically loaded. He takes careful aim, then fingers a trigger.

> JOHNNY
> I love the smell of Napalm in the morning.

> HUGH
> Just keep em' at bay, Johnny!

BOOM! The tank fires towards the APC. It explodes in a massive fireball engulfing the city streets.

> JOHNNY
> Oops...My bad!

The tank rolls on with impunity...

EXT. MAGNUS HQ BUILDING - NIGHT
The building is under heavy lockdown. Soldiers are placed all around the high-rise at every access point. It's an even denser blockade than the one in the streets and firing the cannon would bring them all right down on our trio.

INT. TANK - SAME
Hugh points at a street corner two blocks away from the high-rise.

                    HUGH
          Stop there.

The Tank Driver brings the tank to a halt. Hugh still has the man's gun. He pats the Tank Driver on the shoulder.

                    HUGH (CONT'D)
          Thanks for all your help. You don't know it yet, but you
          just helped save the world.

As they all exit the tank via the underbelly hatch, the Tank Driver sits in his seat and face-palms.

EXT. CITY STREET - MOMENTS LATER
Hugh finds a manhole cover in the street, and pulls it open.

                    GRACE
          Not exactly where I thought we'd spend our second
          date.

                    HUGH
          Won't be a second date if we're all mauled by hungry
          zombies.

GRACE

Fair point.

Grace goes in.

JOHNNY

We don't even know what's down there.

HUGH

Quit bitchin' and get down there.

Johnny sucks in a breath and climbs down. Hugh follows, closing the manhole behind him.

INT. SEWERS - MOMENTS LATER

The sewer is a brick-and-mortar tunnel, lit by old and sputtering fluorescent lights. There is a river of sewage running in the middle of the tunnel. Johnny takes care to avoid it, almost slipping but regaining his balance.

HUGH

There should be an access point beneath the building.

They hear RUMBLINGS and guttural MOANS coming from the darkness way down the tunnel and quicken their step.

Further down the sewer, there's a door that is locked by a heavy chain. A placard reads "UTILITY ACCESS, MAGNUS BLDG."

HUGH

Here it is.

Johnny is bleeding a bit worse and has started to shake a bit. His skin is now a light shade of red as he approaches.

JOHNNY

I got this one. Close your ears.

They earmuff themselves as -- BANG! Johnny pulls a pistol and blasts the padlock away. The POP of the gunfire and the CLANG against the metal padlock echo violently through the tunnel. The GROANS seem louder and closer in reaction.

JOHNNY (CONT'D)
(yelling loudly)
Jesus. I did not think that through. Well, door's open -
who wants to go save the world?

Hugh is about to step through the door when ZOMBYTES ATTACK out of nowhere.

Grace is knocked down by one Zombyte as another grabs Hugh from behind as he steps through the door. Hugh kicks backs, knocking the zombies down.

Johnny helps Grace up and pushes her through the door to safety as the Zombytes come back for more.

A Zombyte grabs hold of Hugh, snapping its bloody, melted skin jaws in his face. Johnny fires a bullet into its head, spilling blood all over Hugh's face. But now they are both deafened by the blast.

JOHNNY

Go! Go! Get in there, doc!

Hugh heads towards the door, looks back and sees a Zombyte coming up behind Johnny.

HUGH

Behind you!!

JOHNNY

What? Yeah, I'm right behind you!

Grace looks into the sewer and SCREAMS as Johnny is grabbed from behind by the Zombyte, who bites into Johnny right where the other creature
did.

JOHNNY

AHHHHH!!!!

GRACE

Nooo!!! Johnny!!! Help him!

More zombies are flowing towards them down the sewer. Johnny fends off the
creature on his back and butts him with the gun.

JOHNNY

Go! Don't worry about me. It's time for you to save
the world.

A bloody and trembling Johnny pushes Hugh towards the door as Grace continues screaming. Hugh jumps through then holds his hand out for Johnny.
    Johnny's skin starts to turn. He looks at Hugh and his hand, then Grace's
pleading eyes. And then SLAMS the door shut in front of him. Grace bangs on
the door.

GRACE

No!! Johnny!! Open the door! Don't do this! Johnny!!
We can use the antidote!! Please!!

Hugh grabs her and pulls her away from the door.

                            HUGH
        C'mon Grace. We can't help him now. He made his
        choice. We gotta go.

INT. MAGNUS HQ - BASEMENT - MOMENTS LATER
The basement lab in the Magnus building has become a torture chamber.
Zombytes are chained up or kept in cages. There are gurneys with cut-up
Zombytes splayed out. The living Zombytes are ravenous and raging.

                            GRACE
        We have to go back! We have to save him! We have to...
                    (noticing her surroundings)
        What the hell are they doing down here?

                            HUGH
        I don't know, but at least we have plenty of volunteers
        to test this thing.

A Zombyte screams in his shackles. Hugh backs away in surprise.

                        HUGH (CONT'D)
        This one will do.

He takes out and readies the cure inside an Eden syringe, and walks slowly to
the chained Zombyte.

                        HUGH (CONT'D)
        Easy... easy... I'm just going to give you some Eden,
        okay? Do you want that?

The Zombyte struggles even more, almost drooling for it. Hugh shoots him up
with the cure then backs away. Seconds later, the Zombyte starts screaming and
gurgling.

The cure is taking effect, coursing through its system.

Hugh and Grace step back as the Zombyte writhes and twists, falling to the floor. Its skin is rebuilt from the red and dripping mass to almost normal-looking skin. Its eyes re-dilate, and its body stops pulsating.

What is left is a man in tattered clothes, still chained to the wall who looks like he has a really bad sunburn.

GRACE

Did it work?

Hugh readies his gun, and inches close to the body on the floor. He keeps the gun pointed directly at the body. Beads of sweat drip off his brow, and his heart is pounding.

He's expecting the body to jump out at him. Grace watches expectantly.

Hugh jabs the body with his gun, and the reformed Zombyte stirs as if from a deep sleep.

REFORMED ZOMBYTE

Ugh... what happened?

HUGH

Are you alright?

REFORMED ZOMBYTE

Ughh... I can't move. What's...?

HUGH

Hold still, I just need a sample of your blood.

Hugh pricks him with a syringe.

REFORMED ZOMBYTE

Ow! Who the hell are you?

HUGH

It'll be alright. Grace, Johnny, watch over him. I need
to make sure it worked.

Grace comes to the Reformed Zombyte's side, while Hugh takes the blood sample to a nearby computer station.

It takes only a few seconds to see the cure in the bloodstream attacking and
destroying the tainted Eden, as well as rebuilding the cells in the blood.

REFORMED ZOMBYTE

What happened?

GRACE

You want the long version or the short?

REFORMED ZOMBYTE

...Huh?

GRACE

Okay, short version: everyone's fucked up.

Hugh looks up from the desk.

HUGH

It's working. It's erasing the tainted Eden and rebuilding his cellular structure!

They unchain the Reformed Zombyte, and with some help he gets up to his
feet.

REFORMED ZOMBYTE

I need to take a piss.

                              HUGH
Um, restroom's down the hall.

He turns to leave, but not before looking over his shoulder at Hugh.

                    REFORMED ZOMBYTE (CONT'D)
What a trip, man.

                              HUGH
You're welcome.
                          (to Grace)
Let's get to Katherine's office.

                              GRACE
No! We know it works now, we have to go back down
and save Johnny! We can't just leave him!

                              HUGH
I'm sorry, there's no time. We have to get this done
first. Johnny would want it this way. Come on!

INT. MAGNUS HQ - ELEVATOR - MOMENTS LATER
Hugh and Grace reach floor "49", the executive level. Hugh presses the
"Emergency Stop" button.

INT. MAGNUS HQ - KATHERINE'S OFFICE - NIGHT
Katherine Walsh's executive office is every bit as spacious and elegant as Ted's
office was but there's no time to be impressed.
    They head for Katherine's desk.

                              GRACE
This isn't right. We should've helped Johnny first.

Hugh looks up from the desk.

> HUGH
>
> We've come this far, we have the cure, and now we
> need to get the evidence to clear us and get the cure
> out to the world.

He locates a file marked "Shipping Manifests." Hugh gets up from the desk, exasperated.

> GRACE
>
> And Johnny?

Hugh ignores the question, engrossed in the manifests.

The shipping manifests load on the holographic projector. From the date of the first shipment of Eden, they can see all the technical details.

It was v.1.2.045 that went into full-scale production at a manufacturing plant.

> HUGH (CONT'D)
>
> That's it! It confirms what we found out back home.
> The wrong version was put into production after the
> first round. And look at this...

Hugh scrolls down the manifest to find an authorization certificate, as well as several redacted FDA posts. The name on the authorization?? Walter Steinberg!

> GRACE
>
> Walter?!

> HUGH
>
> My God. I thought Katherine was pulling the strings.
> Why?

There is teleconferencing software open on the computer, so Hugh taps that icon.

> HUGH (CONT'D)
> Let's find out.

Hugh calls up Katherine over the computer.

INTERCUT AS NECESSARY WITH -

INT. KATHERINE'S PANIC ROOM - NIGHT
Katherine looks bored out of her mind until her pocket computer starts beeping with a message for her. She taps it to power it up, and a hologram of Hugh appears.

> KATHERINE WALSH
> Dr. Stephern! You're still alive!

> HUGH (V.O.)
> Cut the crap, Katherine. We know about what happened to Eden.

> KATHERINE WALSH
> I don't know what you're talking--

> HUGH
> I saw the shipping manifest. The formula was swapped for an unstable version, and Walter authorized it.

> KATHERINE WALSH
> Walter? That doesn't make any sense! We locked him out of the Eden project a long time ago!

HUGH

From the looks of it, he's responsible for the Zombytes.

KATHERINE WALSH

Why should I believe any of this?

Hugh decides to tell Katherine the truth.

HUGH

Johnny's gone. They killed your nephew.

KATHERINE WALSH

No!! You're lying!

The look on Katherine's holographic face is more than apparent. She's shocked and begins to sob.

HUGH

He died to save us. And to make sure we get the antidote made and distributed to the world. But we can't do anything without your help. Where is Walter?

Katherine stops crying, turns furious, and gets on the computer.

KATHERINE WALSH

Hold on.

She calls Walter, and his image appears right next to Hugh's holograph. Walter smiles as his holograph appears.

WALTER STEINBERG

Ah, Ms. Walsh. Figured you were zombie meat by now.

KATHERINE WALSH

You bastard! You swapped the Eden Formula! You made these zombies!

WALTER STEINBERG

It was Stephern and Pilaro! Check the news!

KATHERINE WALSH

You killed my nephew!

WALTER STEINBERG

I did no such thing. It's survival of the fittest out there. And let's face it — a sweet kid but your nephew was never exactly one of the fittest.

KATHERINE WALSH

You bastard. How could you do this?

Walter goes silent, then lowers his gaze.

WALTER STEINBERG

Fine... Not much point in being subtle anymore I guess.

ANGLE ON WALT'S HOLOGRAPHIC IMAGE IN KATHERINE'S PANIC ROOM-

WALTER STEINBERG

You and my father took everything from me. Now you know what that feels like. Now the world will know. Don't worry, you won't have too long to be sad. A good friend of mine should be there any minute. Happy Apocalypse, Ms. Walsh.

Walter cuts out, leaving her to talk with Hugh on the holograph. She is stunned and can't even get a word out. Hugh and Grace look almost as heartbroken.

                              HUGH
          Katherine... I'm so--

                      KATHERINE WALSH
          Walter...he needs to pay! Send me everything you've
          got and I'll make sure it gets to the press.

                              GRACE
          You can tell them we have a cure too. We've got a
          handful of syringes full of the antidote. We just need to
          get it into the right hands.

INT. MAGNUS HQ - KATHERINE'S OFFICE - CONTINUOUS
Hugh gathers up the shipping manifests, the log about v.1.2.045 of the formula, and Walter's authorization. He sends them all to Katherine with a quick scan of his phone.

                              HUGH
          Okay, it's all sent.

Katherine regains some of her composure.

                      KATHERINE WALSH
          Go. Get to the lab, get the cure ready. The truth be-
          hind the Eden Formula will come out! Even if it kills
          me too.

They disconnect the phone call.

INT. KATHERINE'S PANIC ROOM - NIGHT
Katherine tries to regain her composure. There are some sounds of clattering around outside the panic room. On the video screen in the panic room, she can see a large MAN enter her house.

INSERT – KATHERINE'S PHONE
She sends all the information from Hugh out to a huge list of people. Then she gets up, takes a deep breath, and opens the Panic Room door.

INT. KATHERINE'S LIVING ROOM - CONTINUOUS
Katherine turns around to find COL. KILPATRICK, in all his intimidating glory, his GUN already by his side.

                    KATHERINE WALSH
        I know what you're here to do. Make it quick.

                    COL. KILPATRICK
        I don't think you have any idea why I'm here.

He holsters his weapon.

                    COL. KILPATRICK
        Is it true they have a cure?

INT. KATHERINE'S OFFICE – SAME

                        HUGH
        We're on our own. We have to get the antidote to the
        lab and into the production system and we have to—-

The big flat screen TV in the office suddenly comes on – and it's Walter!

WALTER (ON TV)

Huuuugh. When will you realize, you can't stop fate. If it wasn't youth-thirsty zombies it would have been something else. A pill that makes you lose body fat but also grow horns and kill puppies. Or a drink that makes your hair grow back, but also causes cannibalism. Ever notice how many side effects are listed in a commercial for medicine? But do people care? No! Because getting an extra centimeter on their eyelashes is more important.

Face it, Hugh, you're fighting a battle whose victims don't want to win. Because if they did, they'd just have to stare at themselves in the mirror day after day without any hope of it getting better. I'm doing this country a favor.

GRACE

You're one sick twist.

WALTER

Ah, Gracie. I really should have fucked you when I had the chance. Now I'm just gonna have to kill you.

HUGH

Give it up, Walter. Not even a delusional prick like you can see this ending well for you.

WALTER

On the contrary. After I blow up your precious Elysium labs, I'm headed overseas to launch global production of Eden all over the world. Oh. And I had the military funnel all those poor hungry zombies to Magnus headquarters, the only place to find more Eden. So, those creatures should be tearing this building apart anytime now.

> (beat, genuine)
> Hugh, this doesn't have to end this way. We're friends.
> I'm willing to take you with me. Both of you. Join me
> and we can make billions. Chopper leaves in 10 min-
> utes. That gives you enough time to either leave with
> me and escape with your lives or try to get to the lab
> in one piece in a feeble attempt to save a world blind to
> its own flaws.

The TV goes black.

> HUGH
> (to Grace)
> I've got to stop him.

Grace goes to the window and looks out across the landscape of a broken and bloody Los Angeles.

Then down at the outside of the Magnus Building, where hoards of Zombytes are making their way towards the building.

EXT. MAGNUS BUILDING – SAME

Hundreds of blood-thirsty zombies run towards the Magnus Building and tear through the NATIONAL GUARD and COPS trying to stop them.

It's a blood bath as soldiers try to shoot as many as they can, but are quickly overtaken, bitten torn apart by the creatures. The Zombytes smash their way into the building all chanting "EEEDENNN".

INT. KATHERINE'S OFFICE - SAME

> HUGH
> Grace, come on! We have to try. For everything it took
> to get this far. For Johnny. For Katherine. For Ted. For
> the millions of—

                           GRACE
            You had me at Grace. Let's go.

INT. HALLWAY – MAGNUS HQ - CONTINUOUS
Hugh and Grace, armed to the teeth, run as fast as they can through the corridors
of the high rise, trying to make it to the elevator. They're on the 49th floor – the
Elysium lab is a long way down.
     They get to the bank of elevators. DING! They get inside.

INT. ELEVATOR - CONTINUOUS
They stand silent for a moment, that damn Muzak still playing. Until –

                           HUGH
            Quick, take out your phone. We need to record a mes-
            sage. Something to let people know there's a cure.

She begins recording.

                           HUGH
                        (on camera)
            Um, I'm Dr. Hugh Stephern and I have a message for
            the people affected by Eden. We have a cure! Believe
            me when I say that what happened to Eden was not
            our doing. The formula was tampered with by Magnus
            CEO Walter Steinberg, whom I also believe had his
            father killed. We can help you. But first we need to –

CRASH!!! The top of the elevator is smashed in as a Zombyte drops down. The
elevator STOPS suddenly. Grace drops her phone, but quickly recovers.
     The creature goes after Hugh, Hugh barely able to hold him off as he hisses
and bites at him.

ZOMBYTE

Eeeeeeeeden!

GRACE

Shoot him!

HUGH

No wait! The antidote. Give him one!

Grace grabs one of the syringes from her pocket and as Hugh holds the creature as still as he can, she plunges the syringe into its neck and empties half the liquid into him.

In seconds, the Zombyte begins to revert back to normal human form. When the Zombyte backs off from Hugh and stares at him in wonderment, Hugh butts him with the gun, knocking him out.

HUGH

It was easier than explaining. Send that video every-where you can.

Grace starts fidgeting with her phone to send it.

Hugh hits the elevator buttons, but it's dead. Stuck.

Hugh pries the doors open and they are stuck between floors. He sees if the coast is clear and then jumps out, taking aim around him with his 9MM. Still quiet, he pulls Grace out of the elevator and they head to the nearby stairs.

INT. STAIRWELL – 25th FLOOR – CONTINUOUS

They enter the stairwell, guns aimed and ready. They begin to make their way down as the MOANS of Zombytes get louder.

Two floors down, a ton of Zombytes pour through the stairway doors on every floor – and they all begin to head UP.

                    HUGH
        Fuck. Looks like we're shooting our way down to the
        lab. Ten floors. Let's do this.

Hugh and Grace are zombie killing machines as they head down the stairwell.
Dozens of zombies converge and Hugh tosses many over the stairwell over the
railing to their deaths.
        BLAM BLAM! Grace shoots zombies left and right, hitting some with the
butt of the gun and kicking them out of the way.
        Hugh FIRES his handgun and uses his rifle to knock their heads around,
but man they keep coming!

                    HUGH
        We're running out of ammo. What do you say we just
        give them what they want?

They get to the landing on Level 19 and Grace hands him a syringe full of the
Eden antidote.
        Hugh holds it up high.

                    HUGH
        Eden!! Is this what you want? Huh? You need your fix?
        I got your shit right here.

The Zombytes are all memorized by the syringe, practically frothing at the
mouth. Actually, they are.

                    HUGH
        From one recovering addict to another, let me tell
        ya... the first one's free. But the next one? It's a fuckin'
        doozy.

Hugh chucks the syringe of Eden (antidote) over the railing and straight down the center of the dizzying stairwell.

The Zombytes hungrily follow after it, with dozens jumping to their deaths down the empty abyss of the stairwell.

HUGH

Guess that's one way to kick the habit.

Grace and Hugh run down the last few levels and exit to the Elysium floor.

INT. ELYSIUM LABS – CORRIDOR – CONTINUOUS
As they exit the stairs to the maze-like Corridors of Elysium, they see Walter across the other side getting out of another elevator. He has what looks like a BOMB device.

HUGH

Son of a bitch. Walter! Stop!

Walter sees Hugh and Grace coming after him and he FIRES at them, the shots chipping away bits of wall nearby. Walter disappears down a different hallway.

Hugh and Grace try to follow, but when they get to an intersection of corridors and take a right turn, they find another wave of Zombytes converging on them.

They try to double back, but more Zombytes are coming from the left.

Back to back, they reload their chambers, and begin to shoot their way through the carnage and bloodshed as Zombytes attack.

Hugh sees Walter run past towards the labs as he blows away another face-melting monster.

HUGH

That way! Come on!

They run after Walter towards the lab doors but Zombytes get there first and jump at Grace and Hugh when –

BLAM! BLAM! BLAM! BLAM! BLAM! BLAM!

Down they go in a hail of bullets. And when they fall, we can see the high powered machine gun is attached to Colonel Kilpatrick.

> COL. KILPATRICK (CONT'D)
> Heard you two have a cure for these things. I think it's time the world finds out.

> HUGH
> Walter Steinberg's in the lab. He's the one—

> COL. KILPATRICK
> Oh, I know all about it.

But just as the three walk in – BAM BAM BAM!

Walter sees them, and shoots right at them. Hugh grabs a Zombyte and takes cover behind the corpse.

Walter's shot hits Grace in the shoulder.

She screams and goes down, clutching her wounded shoulder. Hugh rushes to her aid.

> HUGH
> Grace!

> GRACE
> Stop him!

Walter dives behind a corner into an office room. Hugh gives chase. Kilpatrick goes around the other way.

THROUGH DIFFERENT ELYSIUM LABS/OFFICES -

> WALTER STEINBERG (O.S.)
> So fucking predictable, Hugh! I knew you'd make the wrong choice. But see, I can't let you use that antidote.

> HUGH
> (hides behind office wall)
> Walter! Don't do this!

> WALTER STEINBERG (O.S.)
> Sorry, Hugh. It's the nature of the beast. So to speak. That antidote is not leaving this room. And if you get in my way, neither are you. Anyone who takes Eden deserves what they get.

> HUGH
> How about all the innocent people the zombies killed? What about them?

> WALTER STEINBERG (O.S.)
> Collateral damage, as they say.

> HUGH
> What happened to you, Walt? I thought I knew you.

Hugh searches an office hallway for Walter, gun drawn.

> WALTER STEINBERG (O.S.)
> You always were naive! Thought you could save the world and finally make Daddy love you. Well, it's never going to happen.

Walter shoots at Hugh, and Hugh ducks behind a partition.

> WALTER STEINBERG (CONT'D)
> The world's already goin' to hell! We might as well just burn it down!

A Zombyte stalks towards Hugh, who shoots him down. He peeks around the corner of a lab, sees Walter up ahead.

> HUGH
> <u>You</u> killed all those people!

> WALTER STEINBERG
> Humanity is the real monster. I just proved it!

Walter sees Hugh and shoots at him but Hugh dodges the bullet.

> HUGH
> What about your father? Did you set <u>him</u> up too?

> WALTER STEINBERG
> Don't you dare talk about my father like you really knew him!

Pissed, Walter charges in where he heard Hugh's voice, and starts to FIRE, shattering computers, holographic machines and glassware.

Hugh crawls over some broken glass, gets up, and dodges behind another partition.

> WALTER STEINBERG
> The old man held me back for too long, and I did what I had to do!

HUGH (O.S.)
I looked up to you! You were my friend! I trusted you!

WALTER STEINBERG
There's nothing left, Hugh! It doesn't matter how many discoveries we make or what we cure, nothing will ever really change for the better!

Walter returns to the bank of computers and finishes wiring whatever he is doing and disappears out a side door just as Hugh comes around the corner, gun first. No one there.

He takes off out the side door after Walter, running past whatever device he's left behind.

CLOSE ON COMPUTER BANK –
We see an Explosive Device that reads 5:19... 5:18... 5:17.

LAB FOYER –
Hugh returns back to the front of the lab where Grace was laying, hurt, but now she's gone. Kilpatrick is still nowhere to be seen either.

HUGH
Grace? Where are you? You okay?

WALTER STEINBERG
That depends on you, old friend.

Walter appears from behind a lab door holding a bleeding Grace in one hand and a gun to Grace's head in the other.

HUGH
Let her go.

WALTER STEINBERG
No problem. All you need to do is destroy the antidote.
Now.

He cocks the gun at her head. Grace slowly slides her hand into her pocket with
the syringes. Hugh catches this.

HUGH
Funny thing about the antidote. When infected with
your version of Eden, it works great. But if you're not
infected at all, the antidote has some very unfortunate
side effects. In the wrong hands...

WALTER STEINBERG
It could be exactly what I need to reach those who
are too paranoid to take Eden but still deserve to die.
Maybe your father was right. You really do fail at everything. Hand them over now or she dies.

HUGH
I don't want to kill you!

WALTER STEINBERG
Good. Then I'll just kill you!

Walter turns the gun on Hugh just as Grace pulls her hand up and stabs Walter
in the neck with the antidote syringe, plunging it right into his bloodstream and
running away from him to safety.
    Hugh FIRES, shooting Walter's hand and he drops the gun. His arm goes
up to the syringe, pulling it out of his neck.

> WALTER STEINBERG

You think you won? In 2 minutes, this place will blow and you'll die right alongside me. The antidote will never see the light of day.

> COL. KILPATRICK (O.S.)

You may want to count again.

Kilpatrick walks into the room holding the disarmed and dismantled bomb device.

Walter falls to his knees as he holds his neck. He begins to tremble and spit blood.

> COL. KILPATRICK

You still have enough antidotes to mass produce it?

> HUGH

One vial left. All we need.

Walter start to convulse, his skin begins to turn red, blotchy and blistered. His breathing is more labored and he begins to bleed from different orifices. His eyes go yellow, his skin begins to melt off of him.

> WALTER STEINBERG

Save me. I can help you... Please! Huuuuugh! You can't just watch me die. Not when you have a cure... C'mon you worthless junkie fuck!

With that, Hugh raises his gun and blasts Walter in the head, killing the monster...and the Zombyte that used to be his friend.

> HUGH

How's that for a cure?

He turns to celebrate with Grace and notices that Grace is been bleeding profusely and looks pale as a sheet.

> HUGH

Grace?!

She suddenly falls down in a heap.

F
A
D
E

O
U
T

.

FADE IN:

INT. HOSPITAL ROOM - DAY

Grace rests in a hospital bed with Hugh at her side. Bandages cover her wound and she is still weak. A NURSE changes the bandage, and a DOCTOR is with Hugh.

> HUGH

How is she, Doc?

> DOCTOR

The bullet missed all the internal organs, clean through her shoulder. She'll be fine.

Grace stirs, her eyes open. Hugh stays close to her.

HUGH

You're gonna have to stop scaring me like that. I don't know what I'd do if you were gone.

GRACE

Probably have to save the world on your own.

HUGH

It wouldn't be worth saving...I love you, Dr. Pilaro.

Grace smiles. They kiss.

EXT. GRIFFITH PARK – LOS ANGELES - DAY

A huge monument has been erected in Griffith Park to the victims of the 2025 Zombyte Outbreak.

There is a massive ring of polished black stone, etched with the names of all those deceased in the nationwide attack. Among the names listed on the monolith are Johnny Myers and Theodore Steinberg.

Hugh and Grace are there, dressed in black to pay their respects. A Marine plays "Taps" on a bugle while Hugh and Grace each lay a rose next to the monument. Their roses join a large pile of other flowers, rosaries and other mementos of the deceased.

EXT. WHITE HOUSE LAWN - AFTERNOON

PRESIDENT THOMAS SECORD speaks on the White House Lawn in front of members of Congress, guests (including Katherine), and tons of media.

PRESIDENT THOMAS SECORD

Human nature has always been difficult for anyone to control. To venture into unknown regions, to discover that which could change life for the better or

worse -- this responsibility has always fallen to coura-
geous men and women. Many of whom have given
their lives for the betterment of us all.

But along the way, we must always be vigilant for
those who would wield this power for selfish gain, and
those who would see innocent lives destroyed without
accountability.

Hugh and Grace are smiling, looking well-recovered from the ordeals of the past
few weeks.

> PRESIDENT THOMAS SECORD (CONT'D)
> Today, we recognize two extremely talented and coura-
> geous scientists who have been through the gauntlet of
> scandal, loss and victory. Formally and rightfully ex-
> onerated of any suspicion in the cataclysmic events of
> the last few weeks, it is through their efforts that we all
> stand here today.
>
> And I am happy to announce that under their direction
> and my command, the recovery operation known as
> Cleansing Breeze is in full effect. My fellow Americans,
> please welcome Dr. Hugh Stephern and Dr. Grace
> Pilaro.

Hugh and Grace rise and walk to the podium to speak.

> HUGH
> Well...

His voice echoes in several microphones. Caught off-guard, he quickly recovers.

HUGH (CONT'D)

My uncle, Dr. Henry Golden, had the dream of bringing eternal youth to the world. Not for the superficial reasons, but so families could have more time together. So people could live healthier, longer, happier lives. And despite the heinous actions of a few in the last few weeks, I still have faith that his dream will come true.

I feel the loss of the nation on my conscience and wish things could have been different. But thru meeting some truly heroic people like Ted Steinberg and Johnny Myers, I know that we are a strong and resilient people who will continue to heal and see the importance of scientific exploration to our future. Thank you.

GRACE

As far as Cleaning Breeze is concerned, the cure is being produced in an aerosol form and sprayed on every city around the country. In addition, individual injection doses are available at most major hospitals, free of charge. Reports have shown ninety-three percent decreased Zombyte activity, and those numbers are getting better every hour. Plus with the help of Elysium CEO, Katherine Walsh, almost 99% of the supply of the poisonous formula has been accounted for or destroyed. We anticipate soon that there will be no more Zombytes left in the country.

The crowd applauds, and Hugh and Grace embrace.

The President turns to the two scientists, and presents them each with a golden medal on a blue strip of fabric, placing them around their necks.

PRESIDENT SECORD
And with that, Dr. Hugh Stephern and Dr. Grace Pilaro,
I hereby present you with the Congressional Medal of
Honor, the highest honor our nation can bestow.

The crowd cheers as they receive their medals. Hugh takes the podium again.

HUGH
Excuse me, Mr. President. But if I may, I have one
more important thing I need to say.

Grace is taken aback. The President gives him the podium. Hugh turns to Grace,
still with microphones on him.

HUGH (CONT'D)
Grace, after everything we've been through, you have
made me a better scientist and a much better man and
I want to be in this experiment called life with you for
as long as we live. Will you marry me?

Grace can't believe it, and after a beat --

GRACE
Yes.

They embrace and kiss right there in front of the podium, with cheering crowds
all around them.

ON CROWD –
Within the audience is revealed Hugh's father, Morgan, who cracks a smile for
the first time and slowly stands up and claps with everyone else.
    As Hugh and Grace embrace, Hugh sees his father in the crowd. Their eyes
meet, they nod, and Hugh knows he's finally earned the respect he's sought.

FADE OUT

AS CREDITS ROLL –

FADE IN -

INT. WALTER'S PENTHOUSE APARTMENT - DAY

Annie is still passed out on his couch. She suddenly wakes up, tons of empty bottles, paraphernalia and drugs all over the place. She clears the cobwebs and looks around, confused as to what day it even is.

> ANNIE
>
> Hello? Walt? Anyone here?

When she doesn't get any response, she searches the tables for some unused drugs. She looks under the coffee table and her eyes light up. She reaches down, grabs something and injects it (O.S.) into her veins. She has an orgasmic look on her face as she falls back onto the couch.

Moments later, we see her begin to tremble and twitch.

It's only then that we see on the table – an OLD EDEN SYRINGE.

CUT TO BLACK

AT CREDITS END –

FADE IN –

INT. SEWER – DAY

We HEAR GROANS and MOANS throughout the darkened sewers. Bodies of dead Zombytes litter the tombs periodically.

Suddenly, a manhole cover opens above, letting in a sharp beam of bright light. All we see is a pair of feet climbing out of the sewer and into the light.

EXT. SEWER – CONTINUOUS

We rise up from the open manhole cover to the pair of dirty disgusting feet, up, up, up to reveal...Yep...A much more normal and healed looking -

JOHNNY

Heeeeere's Johnny!

CUT TO BLACK

ABOUT THE AUTHORS

About the Author: Born Dominic Rocky Daniels, in the city of Anaheim, California in 1984, he was raised in San Gabriel, CA. At a young age his passion has always been in films, animation, and storytelling. He is best known for his dark fantasy / vampire book series: <u>*The Damascus Chronicles*</u> *(Book 1)* & *The Damascus Chronicles: Denizens of the Night (Book 2)*, which has won the *Amazon Editors Choice Award: Best Books of 2014*.

Trained in fine art at the age of 10, he decided to go into the entertainment business and become a writer. He is a self-taught author and electronic dance music arranger under his Nega Blast X music production brand. He has a Bachelor Degree of Science in Media Arts and Animation from The Art Institute of California-Los Angeles. In his spare time he reads graphic novels and studies movies, his favorite music is heavy metal.

Website:

www.dominicrdaniels.com

About the Author: Born Douglass Killgore Owen in Gainesville, FL in 1984, he was raised in Gainesville and in Altadena, CA. From the days of his early youth, his fascination for creating video games and reading science fiction and fantasy novels drove him to become a writer. He works in the video game industry as a professional quality assurance game tester and has worked on a span on many titles which include: *Boom Blox, Command and Conquer: Red Alert 3, Boom Blox Bash Party* and *God of War 2*. He is a fellow graduate of The Art Institute of California-Los Angeles with a Bachelor Degree of Science in Game Art. In his spare time he attends the Los Angeles Saber Guild with fellow Star Wars light saber enthusiasts.

Website:

www.dougowen.com